Billionaire
Untamed

THE BILLIONAIRE'S OBSESSION
Tate

J. S. SCOTT

F
Sco

Billionaire Untamed

Copyright © 2015 by J. S. Scott

Editing by Faith Williams – The Atwater Group
Proofread by Alicia Carmical – AVC Proofreading
Cover by Cali MacKay – Covers by Cali

ISBN: 978-1-939962-56-0 (Print)
ISBN: 978-1-939962-53-9 (E-Book)

Contents

Chapter 1

ind and seduce Marcus Colter.

Lara Bailey's single-minded goal thrummed through her head as she swirled a straw in her untouched glass of iced tea. Her eyes roamed around the luxurious bar of the Rocky Springs Resort. Her first day here in the Colorado winter vacationer's paradise had been an epic fail. She hadn't once spotted Marcus, the eldest of the iconic, billionaire Colter siblings, and she hadn't even been able to find out his whereabouts.

All she'd gotten out of today was a lightheaded, unpleasant episode when she headed down to the resort's gym to do her usual, stringent workout this morning, obviously brought on by lack of adjustment to the altitude here in the high country of Colorado.

Brilliant. She had slowed down her workout for the day and started to drink as much water as possible. It was critical that she didn't have any weaknesses right now, and she needed to adjust to the altitude as quickly as possible. She had started to feel better already, so she guessed her flatlander body was making the adjustments to being somewhere in the middle of the front range of the Rocky Mountains.

Looking around, all she could see was a sea of people who looked as if they'd just come off the ski slopes. Their faces were red from the cold, and they were dressed mostly in ski gear: ski jackets, ski pants, sweaters and scarves. Some of them even had their skis propped against the wall as they chatted with a warm drink in hand.

What would it be like to be one of those vacationers? At the age of thirty, I can't even remember taking a vacation, or when I last did anything just for the fun of it.

Lara felt out of place in a black cocktail dress, especially considering it was barely four o'clock in the afternoon. But she had a mission, and she was dressed for the goal she wanted to complete. She crossed her long, slender legs, casually flipped her dark blonde hair over her shoulder, and surveyed the people as her mind worked frantically on another plan.

If I can't find Marcus Colter, I'm going to have to make him come to me somehow.

Honestly, Lara would rather be almost anywhere else other than where she was right now—what looked to be a big, fabulous playground for the wealthy. She hated the flirty dress and power heels she wore: footwear that had nearly made her fall on her ass as she exited the elevator and caught the thin heel of her shoe in the small metal opening that accommodated the sliding door. Luckily, she'd been alone in the elevator and no one had seen her not-so-graceful entrance into the lobby.

Thank God nobody saw me. I need to act like I'm perfectly comfortable here—even though I'm not. I need to find Marcus Colter. But I'd really rather be home in my tiny apartment with several containers of Chinese food, a good book, and something chocolate right now.

She was starving, but she'd taken one look at the menu prices outside the swanky resort restaurant and nearly choked. Dinner would have to wait until she could drive into town.

The price of a basic room here in the resort was bad enough: one night cost more than her entire rent for a month. It wasn't that she *couldn't* pay for dinner here; she didn't *want* to do it. More than likely, she'd still be hungry when she left the eatery. The fancy place looked like one of those restaurants with expensive, tiny portions that wasn't about to satiate her hunger. Lara didn't give a shit about the presentation of her dinner; she cared about whether the food was plentiful and good...or not. It irritated her when she left a restaurant with her purse a whole lot lighter and her stomach was still growling. What good was a pretty plate and a yummy aroma if she only got a few bites for an astronomical price?

There isn't much reason to hang out here much longer. Time to change my clothes and head into town for dinner.

Obviously, the eldest Colter sibling didn't hang out much here at the resort. Apparently none of the Colters did. At the very least, she'd hoped to bump into Marcus's mother, Aileen Colter, a woman who was said to spend a lot of time managing the resort. Unfortunately, she hadn't got a glimpse of one single Colter all day. And she'd recognize every one of them by sight, even if she wasn't personally acquainted with a single one of them. She'd studied plenty of pictures of this particular wealthy family.

"I'd buy you a drink, but it doesn't look like you've done much with the one you already have." A low, sexy baritone reverberated behind Lara, surprising her enough that she had nearly knocked over her glass.

Startled because the man had approached her from behind, Lara turned as she finally spotted a guy she wouldn't mind speaking with: *Tate Colter.*

The stats that she'd memorized about him snapped quickly into her brain: Thirty-one-year-old male, blond hair, gray eyes, six foot one inches, exemplary military record in the Special Forces until some kind of accident had required him to leave the military with an honorable discharge. Maddeningly, she hadn't been able to get too much more information on Tate. He was a billionaire—like every other damn Colter in the family—and was the driving force that had made Colter Fire Equipment the biggest producer of firefighting and fire safety gear in the world. The company was under the Colter conglomerate, but Tate had made it his personal mission to manufacture more sophisticated equipment than any other corporation, had been the man to drive the company into the stratosphere of success.

She hadn't found anything negative in his information. Hell, he was even a volunteer firefighter.

Lara eyed him warily as he moved to the other side of the small table. He looked harmless enough. In fact, he looked amazing in real life—better than his pictures. His blond locks were still as short as they'd been in the photos she'd viewed, but he had a serious case of bedhead today, and some of his hair spiked in various directions. Lara was willing to bet the messy look had come from a hat considering it was the dead of winter in Colorado, and she grudgingly admitted that she kind of liked the fact that he wasn't vain enough to fix it. The just-rolled-out-of-bed look of his hair, and the dimple she could see as he shot her an unassuming grin, made him dangerously attractive.

I've seen better-looking men. The defensive thought popped into her head, probably because of the shiver of awareness that slithered down her spine as she looked at Tate Colter. She *had* seen men more conventionally attractive, but none quite as compelling as the man she currently surveyed cautiously. Dressed casually in jeans, boots, and a green sweatshirt, he should have looked ordinary and drab in his surroundings, but he didn't. Lara knew she needed to proceed with caution no matter how unassuming or nice he appeared to be. Tate Colter had a genius IQ, just like the rest of his siblings. His unassuming smile and boyish grin hid a mind that was assessing her, just as surely as she was checking him out and evaluating his motives.

"I don't accept drinks from strange men anyway," she told him standoffishly. She didn't really want him to go away right now. He might be able to provide her with *some* information, but she didn't want to encourage him either. Marcus Colter was her main interest, but his brother might be able to help her find him.

Tate took the wooden chair, turned it around, and straddled it as he made his enormously fit, muscular body comfortable across from her. "Then I guess we need to get to know each other," he answered in a self-confident tone, as though she was obviously going to comply and fall at his feet in gratitude.

Arrogant lug!

Lara made her expression stay neutral. "Maybe I don't want to know you. Maybe I'm married or have a boyfriend," she hedged.

Tate shrugged. "I didn't say I wanted to fuck you. I just said I wanted to get to know you." He rested his forearms on the back of the chair, still grinning at her mischievously. "Tate Colter." He held his hand out to her over the table. "You looked lonely over here all by yourself."

"Lara." She reluctantly shook his hand quickly and drew her arm back to her side, intentionally giving him as little information as possible. His hands were rough and callused; he didn't have the soft, manicured fingers she'd expect from a billionaire. In fact, he wasn't anything like she'd expected an ultra-wealthy guy to be. He seemed so…earthy, more of an outdoor, active guy than a man who would be perfectly comfortable in a custom suit in a boardroom.

In all likelihood, he's comfortable just about anywhere.

Unfortunately, there were only certain social situations where she felt at home, and just that brief, casual contact with Tate had set off a spark of electricity that raced down her spine.

"I wasn't and am not the least bit lonely. I came here to…think," she said hastily. "Alone."

Tate looked around doubtfully. "This isn't exactly a peaceful thinking place, or a good spot to be alone with your thoughts."

Damn. No, it wasn't. The bar was crowded, noisy, and anything but a place to think. It was a venue to socialize.

"Maybe I just wanted to sit here by myself for a while," she said impatiently, wanting to get any information that would be useful to her and get away from his smoky, probing gray eyes that hadn't seemed to leave her face since he sat down. He made her uncomfortable in a way that she'd never been with a guy before. She'd been with plenty of not-so-nice, attractive men, but it wasn't an evil vibe she got from Tate Colter. It was more like…sinful.

"So are you here on vacation?" Tate asked conversationally, completely ignoring her aloof demeanor.

"Yes." Lara looked back down at her drink and watched the pieces of ice get smaller as she stirred the drink yet again. She didn't want to blow Tate off completely, but she didn't want to say anything to embolden him either. Lord knew the guy was already bold enough. *Be friendlier, but not too friendly.* Lara wanted information from Tate Colter, but for some reason he put her on the defensive. Her instincts screamed at her to run away from him as quickly as possible. The problem was, she couldn't really figure out why.

"I haven't seen you around. When did you get into town?"

"Late last night." God, she wished he'd quit staring at her like a specimen under a microscope. "So you're a Colter?" Lara tried to give him her not-so-smart blonde expression. "One of the famous Colter family?" Flattery worked almost every time.

"I'm not the most famous, but I'm the smartest of the bunch," he told her deadpan, almost as if he was giving her some kind of warning. "My mom is out of town visiting my aunt and uncle, so I promised her I'd stop in every afternoon to make sure everything was okay here. I was just getting ready to leave when I saw you sitting here all by yourself. I definitely feel like it's my job to make sure all of the guests are having a good time since Mom's not around."

As Lara eyed him suspiciously, she wasn't so certain that his arrogant statement wasn't accurate. The cocky self-assurance he exuded in abundance made him incredibly appealing, and she had no doubt he was intelligent. Just short of obnoxious, he *was* definitely brash.

"Don't you have brothers?" she asked, trying to still look ignorant and only mildly interested.

Why do I have this feeling that he's on to me?

The conversation was general, but she felt as though they were playing a hidden game of cat and mouse, and unfortunately she felt very much like the rodent right now.

"And a sister," he answered nonchalantly. "My sister, Chloe, is the baby, a local vet here in Rocky Springs now, and I have three older brothers."

"I remember hearing about twins." She plastered a falsely puzzled expression on her face.

"My two oldest brothers, Marcus and Blake, are identical twins. Blake is a US Senator. Zane is a year older than I am. He's a research doctor in biotechnology."

"And what does Marcus do?" she asked in what she hoped was a casual voice.

Tate shrugged his muscular shoulders. "He travels. He heads most of the business for the whole Colter Corporation."

"That must be difficult to have him away all the time." *Damn, I hope Marcus is here now.* "You don't get to see him very often."

"We're all used to it. Most of us are usually gone for long periods of time, except for Chloe. She's home to stay now. Marcus is coming back to stay for a while tomorrow. He's been gone on business for a while. Zane is in Denver, playing the mad scientist, and Blake should be around soon enough after Congress closes their session for a break." Tate's voice was conversational, but he wasn't smiling anymore, and he watched her face.

He knows I'm digging for information. Damn. Damn. Damn. Why couldn't he be a little less observant?

Lara smiled at him weakly. "That's nice," she answered, putting only casual interest in her tone.

Bingo!

Marcus Colter would arrive in Rocky Springs tomorrow.

"So what are your plans while you're staying with us?" Tate asked, as if he had every right to know her schedule. "Where are you from? What are you running away from?"

"Why do you think I'm running away from anything?" she asked carefully, keeping her answers evasive.

"Isn't that why people take vacations?"

"I'm visiting from the East Coast. I thought Colorado would be a nice change. I work in mortgage banking. It's a stressful job." She shot him a pleasant smile.

"Have you been in the hot springs yet? They're guaranteed to take away stress."

"No."

"Went skiing today?"

"I don't ski," she admitted reluctantly.

"We have lessons. I'd actually be more than happy to teach you myself," he told her in a low, *fuck-me* voice that spoke of more than showing her a few skiing moves.

Lara shuddered as their gazes met and locked. Tate made it perfectly clear that he'd like to teach her more than basic skiing. A lot more.

I got what I wanted. Time to run. Literally.

"Thanks," she said gratefully. "But I'm here to spend some time alone. I actually just broke up with a guy—a man who cheated on me. I'm kind of licking my wounds. I appreciate the offer, but I really do need some time to myself." She hastily got to her feet and smoothed down her skirt. "Thanks for the chat." She rifled through her small clutch purse to find her room key, and nodded at him politely and dismissively as she pulled it out and closed her bag. "Maybe I'll see you around." *Or not…if I can help it.*

Tate rose to his feet and swung the chair back into place. "Lara?"

She had started to walk away, but turned back. "Yes?"

He strolled up to her, took a lock of her hair between his fingers and stroked it for a moment before he leaned down slowly.

Lara's breath caught as she inhaled the masculine scent of him. He smelled like fresh air, pine, and musky male, and he was intoxicating. He towered over her. Even though she was dressed in three-inch heels, she still felt defenseless with him this close to her, and she felt suddenly vulnerable in a way she never had before. Not afraid, but definitely exposed.

For a moment, she thought he was going to kiss her, but he didn't. His lips came to rest next to her ear, and he told her in a husky voice, "Any man who would stray from your side doesn't deserve a second thought." He straightened and lightly grasped her chin and turned it upward so her eyes met his. "Don't let any guy fuck with your head. He isn't worth it."

Lara fell into the smoky gray depths of his eyes for a moment, mesmerized. His statement had been emphatic, sincere, and had stirred her soul. It had actually been awhile since she'd had the cheating boyfriend, but he really *had* existed. She hadn't trusted another guy since.

"I-I'll try to remember that," she stammered awkwardly, momentarily drowning in his heated gaze.

Get a grip, Bailey! Remember what you're here for. Keep your eyes on the prize.

"You do that," Tate answered in a raspy voice.

Lara pulled her eyes from his and backed away from Tate before she turned and hurried toward the elevator. Tate didn't follow, but she could feel his stare track her movements as she got into the elevator—thankfully without tripping on her heels this time—and punched in her floor on the panel with more force than necessary. It took everything she had not to look up at him again as the elevator door *whooshed* closed.

Alone in the plush compartment, she leaned back against the wall and let out a shaky sigh of relief.

What in the hell just happened?

She had an objective, a purpose, and Tate Colter wasn't part of that design. Having gotten what she wanted, Tate was of no further use to her. He was a man to now be avoided.

Marcus was her target, and she needed to make certain that all of her attention was focused on the eldest Colter sibling. She needed to wheedle her way into Marcus Colter's affections.

The elevator *pinged* when it reached her floor, and she hurried to her room, escaping inside with her composure intact and her goal firmly back in focus again.

She actually just blew me off.

Tate's dimple showed in his cheek as he grinned like an idiot, still standing in the spot where Lara had left him. It wasn't often—okay, it was pretty much never—that any woman didn't throw herself at him, even the married ones. And it had been way too long since he'd been interested.

She's not married. Some idiot was stupid enough to let her get away.

It probably should have bothered him that she had basically snubbed him, but he was actually amused. Women didn't rebuff him, especially when they knew exactly who he was. He was a single Colter male, a billionaire, and a reasonably attractive guy. He wasn't accustomed to women running in the other direction rather than trying to get his attention.

He'd watched Lara for a while, enchanted when he'd seen her stumble out of the elevator because of her high heels—after he knew she wasn't going to trip and hurt herself. She'd rallied quickly, and Tate noticed how she surveyed her surroundings alone. Lara wasn't stupid, and Tate already sensed she was here for a reason other than just a vacation. She seemed very alert, almost too aware of her environment for a woman who was supposed to be on vacation.

There was a mystery to be solved with Lara from the East Coast, and strangely enough, he wanted to figure out exactly what she was doing here in the middle of nowhere.

She didn't ski.

She wasn't interested in the hot springs.

Yet, she'd picked Colorado for a vacation?

Was she really nursing a broken heart? Would Rocky Springs really be a place any woman would pick to do that? She didn't seem intent on enjoying *any* of the resort amenities or activities.

Hell, he'd think a warmer climate or a more exciting vacation destination would be a better place to heal a wounded heart. Most people came to Colorado in the dead of winter for only one reason: winter sports. There was no other reason to put up with the brutal temperatures and the almost constant snowfall. If he didn't love the high he got out of his winter sports, his family, and his home state so much, he'd probably be on a nice tropical island somewhere himself right now. Lara was alone and didn't seem interested in the springs *or* winter sports, so what was she really doing here?

The *do-me* dress she'd worn made no sense either. It didn't exactly invite solitude. But if she was trying to attract a man, why had she been so quick to get rid of him?

All it had taken was a split second of vulnerability he'd seen in her eyes that told him she was being truthful about the cheating boyfriend. But was that really why she was here now? She looked out of place, different from the usual lighthearted vacationers and skiers who were here this time of year. And he *had* gotten the impression that she *was* running away from something or someone.

Me?

His grin grew even larger as he walked out of the bar. She *had* walked away from him quite easily, never looking back, and *that* intrigued him. It made him all the more determined to know her... and to fuck her.

I lied when I said I didn't want to fuck her. He *did* want her...had wanted her since the moment he saw her tripping out of the elevator.

It had been a long time since he'd desired a woman like he wanted Lara—since way before his accident. His cock had been as hard as a rock from the minute he caught a glimpse of her, and his blatant arousal wasn't going away. She was beautiful, with long blonde hair, soulful brown eyes that seemed to hide a thousand secrets, a gorgeous body that he itched to explore. Her slender legs seemed to go on forever, and there was nothing he wanted more than to have them wrapped around his waist as he pounded into her. They would both be left sated and satisfied.

It had taken all the strength he had not to wrap those silken strands of hair around his hand and taste those plump, gorgeous lips of hers right here in the bar.

But I will taste her. Soon.

She might not land in his bed tonight, but Tate could wait. He was an expert at waiting, picking exactly the right moment to act. She'd definitely be worth it.

I need to find out more about Lara from the East Coast with a stressful job and an asshole for an ex-boyfriend.

That was all he knew about the woman who had aroused his interest and his cock, except for the fact that she was a guest at the resort, but it didn't matter. He *owned* part of the resort, so getting access to her information wasn't a problem. Hell, getting any information about her wasn't an issue. All it would take was a phone call.

He planned his strategy as he made his way to the reception desk to learn whatever he could about the woman who had brought his libido back with a vengeance.

It had been so long since any woman had awakened his interest, much less his cock, and they both felt pretty damn good. Lara stimulated both, and he knew no other woman was going to do for him now that he'd met her. He wanted *her*, and he was going to get her, even if he had to play dirty. It had been too damn long since he'd scratched that itch, and now that a woman had brought back his desire for carnal pleasure, he wasn't letting her get away. She wanted him, too. He could sense it. But something held her back. It wasn't a game for her, and she wasn't playing hard to get. She'd truly meant to give him the cold shoulder, ignore him.

Not. Happening.

Tate shot a killer smile at the hotel receptionist and moved behind the counter to access the computer for the resort.

Tate didn't accept failure well. Never had. He'd have a plan in place before the night was over, his sole objective to get Lara into his bed as soon as possible.

If her heart was really broken, he'd fix it in the most pleasurable way imaginable.

Chapter 2

L ara let out an audible yawn as she took the separate elevator from her room that led to the resort gym the next morning. Her stomach rumbled for her breakfast. She'd managed to get into the town of Rocky Springs the night before and found a small family restaurant. The two double bacon cheeseburgers and chili cheese fries she'd consumed last night had worn off, and she was starving.

Workout first.

In a pair of black yoga pants and a gray T-shirt, her hair confined in a ponytail at the back of her head, she was ready to get her workout done quickly. She slugged down the last of her coffee that she'd made in the room and dropped the cup into a trashcan outside the gym. It was early morning, and she expected the gym to be deserted like it had been yesterday morning.

She was wrong.

The door was propped open, and Lara peeked into the large gym, surprised to see a young couple on the large, padded mat in the middle of the room. The brownish-haired man was tall and slender, sporting a white judo gi with a black belt cinched around his waist. The female, dressed similarly to Lara, she recognized as Chloe Colter.

Lara moved closer to the door as she heard the sound of distress in Chloe's voice. "James, you're hurting me."

The man had a hold on the smaller woman's wrist as he said arrogantly, "You said you wanted to share some of my interests, Chloe. Martial arts require some pain and discipline."

Lara rolled her eyes and gritted her teeth as she watched him deliberately twist the woman's wrist in the guise of showing her some moves. The bastard apparently enjoyed his sadistic twist to teaching—something that was obviously apparent to Lara that he wasn't even qualified to do. He tossed Chloe to the ground with more force than necessary without giving her a reason, or actually teaching her anything.

The bastard just enjoys hurting her. He's not teaching Chloe a damn thing except pain. The asshole must have a mail-order black belt.

Chloe yelped. "We have to stop. I hurt my back. I don't understand how to do this."

Understandable, considering the asshole teaching her wasn't really instructing. He was punishing.

"Get up, Chloe. You'll hurt more than once before you understand," the man said impatiently. He practically yanked Chloe's arm out of the socket as he forced her to stand. "You said you wanted to lose some of that fat off your body before we get married."

Lara flinched. Oh, God. *This* was Chloe Colter's fiancé? Unbelievable! He was a major jerk.

"I do want to lose some weight," Chloe answered dejectedly, a hand to her sore back.

Lara watched in horror as the tall man tossed Chloe again, harder this time.

"Ouch!" Chloe's outcry was one of real pain. "James, I can't do this."

As Chloe's fiancé reached for the smaller woman's arm again, Lara exploded into action. The guy was a damn sadist. Chloe Colter wasn't fat, and her fiancé was a pain-loving bully. What the hell was she doing with a jackass like him? Not only was Chloe pretty, but she was also rich and educated.

Lara hastened to the mat and gently helped Chloe up. "You can watch," she whispered to the dark-haired woman as she steered her away from the mat and off to the side. "Teaching shouldn't be painful," she said in a louder voice. "And you should learn something every time you're bested. A good instructor will start with the basics, and it shouldn't be horribly uncomfortable." She wanted James to hear her last statements, and she let her disdain for the teaching techniques of the man on the mat leak into her voice.

"Who in the hell are you?" His voice was angry and arrogant.

"I'm a guest who doesn't like your teaching strategies," Lara retorted fiercely as she turned to face him.

"James, she's a guest. We should go. I didn't think anyone would be down this early. We don't belong here when there are guests present," Chloe said adamantly from the sidelines.

"You're just afraid of being thrown again," James mocked Chloe.

Hell yeah, she is afraid. You're making her that way...asshole.

"She's hurting. It's not appropriate for you to continue," Lara told him sharply. She could also tell him he was a lousy damn teacher and a cruel jerk, but she kept her tongue. Instead, she suggested, "Why don't you show her how it's done? Examples might help." Lara gave him a saccharine sweet smile.

"I'd happily show her with you," James answered with a vicious smirk.

It was exactly what she was hoping for, and Lara took up her stance. "Show me." She wiggled her fingers for him to come and get her.

He came at her roughly and grasped her arm so tightly that she winced. But she used her center of gravity and her own strong grip on his arm to flip his body end over end, leaving him stunned and gasping for breath on his back on the mat.

"You bitch," he growled menacingly. He rose to his feet, his face red with fury.

"What's the matter, pussy?" she purred. "Don't like picking on somebody with some skills?" It had been a clean throw, and he had no reason to be pissed. However, he was obviously a man who didn't like to be shown up by a woman. He was the type who liked to be the victor—always.

"James, no!" Chloe screamed.

Lara was ready as he attacked her from the back, no longer even trying to pretend he was practicing any kind of martial arts. He was coming in to punish, and Lara already had his number. If he wasn't playing fair anymore, neither was she. As he wrapped an arm around her throat, she let her elbow fly and nailed him in the solar plexus. Just for good measure, she stomped her sneakered foot into his instep and let her fist fly backward to hammer it into his nose.

He let her go and went slowly to the floor with a horrific bellow. "You broke my goddamn nose."

Panting with fury, Lara reacted instinctively as another restraining, male arm came around her shoulders. She flipped the big body behind her over her head, but unlike James, this newcomer didn't release his hold. She found herself hurtling over his body. The two of them rolled over each other and grappled for supremacy. Also, unlike James, this man was good, and he had her subdued in seconds in a hold that wasn't meant to hurt her, but to make her submit. She raised her knee as he held her body beneath his, but he blocked her attempt.

"Sweetheart, before you try to nail a guy in the nuts, you should make sure you can get away," Tate Colter rasped in her ear, his muscular body on top of hers. "Settle down. I wasn't trying to hurt you. I was trying to keep you from trying to kill the novice over there." Tate jerked his head toward James.

Her heart still hammering with adrenaline, Lara nodded. Her eyes locked with Tate's. "What are you doing here?" she panted heavily, her breath sawing in and out of her lungs frantically.

Out of the corner of her eye, Lara saw Chloe help James up and take him out of the gym. Her fiancé glared at Lara as Chloe led him away.

"I came to work out," he answered. His gray eyes swirled with emotion, his body tense. "I didn't think I was going to walk into a brawl this early in the morning. What the hell happened?"

"Can you let me go?" she requested breathlessly.

"Depends. Are you going to try to kick my ass again?" His eyes lit with devilish humor. "You're good, baby. You even know how to fight dirty. But I'm better."

He *was* better, and that annoyed Lara. Tate Colter had been Special Forces, so she supposed she could give herself a break. He was obviously well trained in more than just judo and Krav Maga.

She inhaled, and his masculine scent enveloped her senses. Lara found herself once again falling into and nearly drowning in the depths of Tate Colter's intense, gray eyes. "I give," she told him hastily. Her core clenched from the body-to-body contact, and she suddenly craved even more than just his muscular body on top of hers. This man made her feel feminine in a way she hadn't felt in a long time…or maybe in a way she'd actually *never* felt before. It was confusing and disconcerting.

She yanked her wrists free of his body and pushed against his chest. "I conceded."

He winked at her. "I know. I'm savoring that."

"Smart ass," she grumbled, relieved when he finally lifted his body from hers and pulled her gently to her feet.

He was dressed simply in a pair of navy sweatpants and a T-shirt that clung to every muscular inch of his chest, arms, abs, and torso. Lara made herself look away and adjusted her own T-shirt distractedly.

"So why did you decide to beat James's ass?" Tate asked curiously.

"He was being mean to Chloe." Lara wandered over to a treadmill and started it at a warm-up speed.

Tate took the treadmill next to hers and hopped on, starting at a walk right beside her. "How did you know who she was?"

Lara thought quickly. "I heard him say her name. She's your sister, right?"

"Yes. My baby sister. What do you mean by saying he was being mean?" His voice grew irritated and menacing.

Lara grabbed the bar in front of her as she walked in place and stared at the painted forest scenes on the wall. "He was inferring she was fat, which she isn't, and he was tossing her to the ground without teaching her anything. She said her back hurt, and he was twisting her wrist for no reason except to make things painful for her. But he wanted to keep on tossing her around, even after she admitted that she was hurting. He's a jackass. Why in the world does she want to marry him?"

Tate shrugged as he sped up his treadmill. "He's a local doctor now, and she's known him since high school. We haven't really seen much of her or him since she graduated from high school except when she was home on break from school. She just graduated from veterinary school last year and started up her own practice here. We're all glad to have her back home. Honestly, I don't think any of us know James very well. I've heard a few rumors about him, but I thought they were just that…rumors. It's a small town."

"If the rumors are saying he's a cruel, sadistic prick, I'd believe them." She increased the speed on her treadmill a little more.

He was silent for a few minutes, as though he contemplated her words. "Believe me, I'll be looking into all of those rumors now. And I'll start watching over Chloe. I think my brothers and I need to have a talk with her. Thanks for helping her out."

She nodded, and there was a comfortable silence for a few moments while they both ramped up their speeds on the treadmills.

"Do you really come here to the resort every day to work out?" Lara asked curiously, wondering why he didn't have a gym in his own home. All of the Colters had houses in Rocky Springs, and they all owned their own acreage. They must have large homes here.

"I mostly come to see Mom every day. I didn't see much of her for years. And then there's the breakfast buffet. I don't cook." He shot her a remorseless grin. "The breakfast here is unbeatable, and it's a really tolerable buffet with fresh food. All you can eat."

Lara's stomach growled. "They have a breakfast buffet here?"

"The front desk didn't tell you? It's included for all the guests." He paused before he added, "And a few intruders like me."

Lara grimaced. "To be honest, I didn't give them a chance to tell me much when I got in. It was late and I was tired. I'm starving," she admitted reluctantly.

"How fast can you finish your run?"

Lara cranked up her speed. "Pretty fast. You?"

"Faster than you," he shot back jokingly. "And if I get there first, I won't leave much."

"I'll get done faster." She cranked her run up to full speed. "And I'm a paying guest. You're actually a moocher," she protested, starting to breathe heavier.

"That won't matter if I get the last waffle." Tate ran on the treadmill, but he hadn't even broken a sweat.

"Not happening," she told him adamantly, determined to make it to the food before Tate did.

They finished at the same time, but Tate showered faster and made it to the buffet quicker than she did.

Despite all of his trash talk, Lara had to admit that he was sweet because he made it a point to actually save her some waffles.

Damn, for a small woman, Lara Bailey can eat.

Tate sat across from her at one of the small dining tables in the buffet room and watched her consume her third waffle. She'd already devoured a pile of eggs, sausage, bacon, and toast. Eating those items first hadn't even slowed her down. Finally, she chewed at a more even pace, but she hadn't stopped yet.

He didn't think there was anything sexier than a woman who wasn't afraid to enjoy her food. At first, he wondered whether she could out eat him, but he'd managed to consume an even larger breakfast before he stopped. Lara ate slower and savored her food. Now he was just enjoying watching her. Nearly groaning as she licked maple syrup from her bottom lip and closed her eyes in ecstasy, he sat his fork on his empty plate and stared openly.

Lara was an enigma, yet if he took into consideration what he'd found out about her background, maybe she really wasn't. Unfortunately, he hadn't yet found anything about her that he didn't admire or adore about her. Even the way she ate made him like her even more. His dick practically worshipped her. No picking at her food or a salad for this woman. She ate with enjoyment, consumed her meal as if she didn't know when she'd eat again. And the fact that she could kick some major ass?—pretty damn hot. Unfortunately, there were some things about her that troubled him. Namely, what the hell was she really doing here in Rocky Springs? Now that he was aware that she wasn't a tourist, he was even more baffled.

What Lara had said about the way James treated Chloe also nagged at him. If what she said was true, he needed to get with his brothers and find out whether the rumors about James were true, and find a way to get Chloe away from James for good. There was no way he and his brothers were letting their sister marry an asshole.

"You like your food," he commented neutrally as she finished the last bite of her waffle.

She eyed him carefully. "I do. Do you have a problem with that, Colter?"

"Nope. I like it. I can't stand it when women pick at their food and profess not to be hungry when they actually really are starving."

"You do?" Lara looked at him, perplexed.

Tate looked into her chocolate brown eyes and surveyed her confused expression. "I do."

"My ex used to say I ate like a pig." She placed her napkin and fork gently on her plate before she picked up her coffee mug to finish the beverage.

"I think a woman with a healthy appetite is sexy," he rasped. Watching her eat was like watching her come: a look of complete ecstasy on her face. It just made him want to be the cause of that particular expression himself. "Your ex was a douche."

"Agreed," she answered happily.

She looks so much more relaxed today. Happier than she was yesterday.

Lara was dressed casually in jeans, sneakers, and a dark green sweater that made her eyes look even larger than they already did.

"What are your plans for the day?" Tate hoped it was for her to follow him back to his place and spend the day with him in bed. He needed to fuck this woman so badly that his balls were turning blue. Regrettably, he was doubtful that idea was on her radar.

"I already have plans." She looked deliberately at her watch. "In fact, I have to go." She jumped up as if her ass were on fire. "Thanks for telling me about breakfast." She waved at him as she strode across the room like a woman on a mission—another thing he liked about her.

Tate watched; his eyes narrowed as she disappeared into the elevator. "Go ahead and run away, sweetheart. You won't get very far."

Determined to figure out the mystery that was Lara Bailey, he rose from his chair and followed her.

Chapter 3

"**L**ara!"

The sound of a feminine voice calling her name made Lara stop and turn, even though she was impatient to get outdoors. Chloe Colter rushed across the lobby to meet her, dressed in much the same outdoor gear as Lara wore: ski pants, a sweater, a jacket, gloves and hat slung over her arm. Although Chloe was dressed mostly in red, and Lara wore black.

"I'm so sorry about earlier. I just talked to Tate, and he said you were okay," Chloe said in a rush as she reached Lara.

She and Chloe were about the same height, around five foot four, but Chloe had a more feminine frame than Lara, curves that most men enjoyed. Lara noted the distress in Chloe Colter's gray eyes as their gazes met.

"It's okay. I'm sorry, too. I shouldn't have injured your fiancé." *Even though the bastard deserved it.* "Is he okay?" *Not that I care.* Lara plastered a concerned look on her face as she really hoped James was at home in bed, still whining over his probable damaged nose, sprained foot, and sore back.

Chloe fidgeted nervously. "He's all right, but pretty angry right now. He's mad all the time lately. I don't understand what's wrong with him. He's been acting strange since I got back to Rocky Springs last year."

He's an asshole. More than likely, he'd always been that way, but Chloe hadn't seen her fiancé enough to recognize that he was a jerk while she'd been busy with college. The veterinary program had to be intense. "Did you go to the same college?"

"No." Chloe lowered her eyes. "He's four years older than I am, and he was already done with his undergraduate work when I graduated from high school. We were in separate states after that summer. He was in med school the same year I started undergraduate work at college. We dated during the summer before we both had to go our separate ways for school. We saw each other when we could."

"People change," Lara said cautiously. "Maybe it's time to re-think marrying the guy." It was none of her business, but Lara didn't want to see Chloe Colter married to an abuser. She didn't want to see *any* woman married to an abusive male.

"He apologized. He says he's under a lot of stress," Chloe explained hesitantly.

"That's no excuse. Dump him, Chloe. You're educated, beautiful, and young."

Chloe sighed. "Tate said the same thing."

"I'd listen to him," Lara said emphatically, surprised that she and Tate Colter were actually in total agreement on something.

"I'm definitely giving up trying to learn any martial arts with him," Chloe told her adamantly. "I was wondering if you'd teach me."

Lara cursed the pleading look in Chloe's eyes. She wasn't a teacher. "I don't instruct, Chloe—"

"Please. I'd like to learn," Chloe pleaded.

She opened her mouth again to refuse, but gut instinct slammed into Lara. Maybe teaching this woman some basic moves might someday save her life. "I won't be here very long, but I'll teach you some basic self-defense stuff before I leave."

Chloe looked relieved. "Thank you."

"Are you headed out?" Lara nodded at the winter gear in Chloe's arms.

"Yeah. I want to see if I can catch a few runs on the slopes before the blizzard gets here. We're supposed to get pounded later this afternoon. Once the winds get too high and the visibility starts to suck, they'll close the slopes." Chloe looked Lara up and down. "You look dressed for the outdoors. Do you want to come along with me?"

"I actually don't ski," Lara confessed. "I rented a snowmobile for the day. The trails look awesome." Not that she had any intention of following all of the trails, but the snowmobile paths were pretty extensive around the resort property.

If Marcus Colter won't come to me, I'll go to him.

"Be careful," Chloe told Lara in a warning voice. "There's a blizzard coming in later. Do you know how to handle a sled in mountain terrain? The trails are pretty easy, but it's a little tricky on some of the steeper areas."

"Absolutely." Lara lied through her teeth. It had taken her a minute to realize that the "sled" Chloe was talking about was actually the snowmobile. *Is that what they called them here?* "I'll be cautious, though," she added to make Chloe feel better.

"Good. Have fun." Chloe beamed at her. "Stick to the novice trails and come back before the storm hits."

Lara hadn't even known there *was* a storm coming in. She'd been too involved in her research and finding the exact location of Marcus Colter's home. A snowstorm might actually work to her advantage. Obviously, she couldn't drive onto Marcus's property for no reason. But she could go out on a snowmobile and get accidentally lost, right? A storm comes in and covers the trails, and she ends up at Marcus Colter's home without suspicion. Just a lame, ditzy tourist who gets lost in the mountains.

Perfect.

Lara smiled and waved at Chloe as they exited together and parted ways. Heading straight to her rented snowmobile, she yanked on her outerwear, anxious to finally accomplish the job she'd come here to Rocky Springs to perform. She had to. She was very quickly running out of time.

A few hours later, Lara found out that the challenge of actually riding the snowmobile on mountain terrain wasn't a problem. It had been the unknown, the lack of knowledge of the area that had found her lying on her ass in the snow. Although she hadn't been riding very fast, the pine tree had come out of nowhere when she came up over a slope, and she slammed right into the trunk of the massive obstacle.

"Dammit!" She rolled to her feet, annoyed with herself for rendering her only mode of transportation at the moment disabled. On impact, one of the skis on the front of the transport had broken, and she'd only veered off the trail a mile or so back, meaning she was still several miles from Marcus Colter's home.

"Shit. Shit. Shit," she muttered irritably to herself as she stared at the unfixable ski. "I guess I'll be walking."

The wind speed had increased, and the visibility had started to suck, which was one of the reasons she hadn't been quick enough to avoid the tree. Snow came down heavily now, and her boots were already covered in snow nearly to her knees since she was off-trail.

Find my way back to the trail or continue on to find Marcus's home?

Tearing off her helmet, she took a step toward the snowmobile that she'd flown off of only a few minutes ago. The muscle in her right thigh protested; she winced. She'd hyperextended her leg, the limb getting caught up on the snowmobile and stretched before she had finally been thrown off the vehicle. As she rubbed at the painful, large muscle without relief, Lara knew her safest option was to head back to the trail before it was covered in snow so she could find her way back to the resort.

Diving into the zipper pocket of her jacket, she pulled out her cell phone. "Of course. No signal," she muttered under her breath as she fumbled to slip the phone back into her pocket. If she was in a no signal area, it should pick up as she got closer to the lodge. If the weather caused the outage, she was screwed.

Wishing like hell she hadn't stopped at the sports shop near the resort on her way out to the trails, she limped back toward the snowmobile route. She had a warmer hat, a scarf, and thicker gloves, but a whole lot of good those items were going to do for her now that she was stuck in a blizzard. She would have been better off leaving immediately instead of making the stop for warmer outer gear and then making a phone call to her boss. Those two things had lost her time, and it would have been a valuable hour and a half considering the winter storm had just started. She could have been at Marcus Colter's home by now.

With her scarf over her face to protect it from the brutal wind and snow, Lara made her way painfully back toward the area where she'd left the trail, stopping way too often because her leg was killing her.

Keep going. Just keep moving.

It was too damn cold for her to slow down. And it was getting almost impossible for her to see a damn thing. The landmarks she'd taken note of during her ride were no longer visible. She put her helmet back on, hoping to get better vision with the visor to protect her eyes, but it didn't help.

She was stuck in a total whiteout and stopped to attempt to get her bearings. Refusing to panic, she leaned against a tree and squinted into the swirling mass of white that blocked her vision. That was when she thought she heard the sound of a motor blending with the howling wind.

I'm hearing things. Nobody else is going to be out in this weather.

But the noise got stronger, closer, and Lara waved her arms in the hope that whoever was crazy enough to be out here with her would see her. Fortunately, she wore mostly black snow gear. She should stand out in the whiteout conditions.

Somebody did see her, and Lara was astounded as a powerful, black snowmobile came to a stop right beside her. The person piloting the vehicle was large, probably male, but she couldn't make out any facial features. All she could see was his helmet and the goggles that protected his eyes.

"Get the fuck on the back, Lara. Now."

The mystery of who was out in the storm was solved as she heard the angry male bellow of Tate Colter, his voice loud enough to be heard over the brutal, wailing force of the wind.

She didn't hesitate to admit her relief as she swung her leg over the back of the powerful machine and put her arms gingerly around the powerful body on the snowmobile. It didn't matter that he annoyed her. She was grateful to see anybody on a working vehicle at the moment.

"Hold on tight," he growled in a voice loud enough for her to hear him.

In the end, she didn't have any choice but to hold onto him, nor did she have the opportunity to look for passenger holds to hang onto instead of clinging to Tate. He took off like a bat out of hell the moment she was seated and her feet were in place. The snowmobile he drove was a lot more powerful than the one she had rented. She clung to him; her heartrate accelerated as she wondered whether the guy had a death wish and he would take her along with him. He flew through the blizzard at breakneck speeds that might have been exhilarating if she hadn't been terrified.

How could he see where he was going? All Lara could see was pure white everywhere and she finally ducked her head behind him and lowered it to his back to block the wind, unable to do anything except trust him and keep her death grip around his waist. She tried not to hamper his driving. She attempted to lean with him when she needed to, but it was almost impossible to anticipate his moves until he'd already made them. His lightning-quick actions on the powerful machine were already completed before she could even react.

After the first few minutes, her heartbeat slowed, and her erratic breathing began to normalize as she realized that Tate seemed to know exactly what he was doing.

If we aren't dead yet, he obviously knows what he's doing.

They were surrounded by trees, and they flew up and down slopes without a single mishap. Tate handled the drive as though he'd done it a million times before. She still thought he was insane for traveling so fast in adverse conditions, but he was obviously comfortable with it, completely familiar with the terrain.

Lara shivered, her body half frozen from the intensity of the cold winds.

Her breath hitched as the skis of the snowmobile left the ground and flew over a narrow ditch. Lara finally exhaled as they landed deftly and surprisingly lightly on the other side. They flew downhill for what seemed like the millionth time, and Tate turned the machine onto what was probably a road, a flat tract of land that wasn't covered in as much snow. He gunned the engine and opened the snowmobile up to full throttle as they careened down the flat, open space of land devoid of trees.

She didn't even see the house until they were nearly on top of it. Tate slowed and came to a stop in front of a large log home.

"Get inside and get warm. The front door is open. I have to put up the sled." His voice was powerful and no-nonsense.

Lara didn't argue. She clambered off the back of the machine, hanging onto Tate to compensate for her gimpy leg. As she staggered to the door, she saw him disappear into the haze of white almost immediately.

She turned the knob on the beautiful front door, and it gave easily. She stepped onto the gorgeous wood floor in the foyer, and stripped off her snow gear as quickly as possible. Lara frowned; she wished she had entered in a mud room of some kind. After she gathered up her wet boots, socks, snow pants, jacket, and other saturated winter gear, she veered toward what looked like a kitchen, and passed a lovely, rustic living room with antique fire equipment that decorated the walls and shelves on her way. With her arms full of wet gear, she didn't have time to admire the kitchen, although it was definitely large and looked like any cook's dream. Relieved, she located the laundry room and mud room to the garage off the kitchen. She hung her wet things on the hooks provided and searched the kitchen for a towel. The house was gorgeous, and she didn't want to leave water on the beautiful wood floors. It might be a log home, but it was more of a mansion than a little cabin in the woods. Everything was custom, the detail put into the construction evident in every wooden beam adorning the ceiling to the luxurious wood floors. It was interesting how the builder had managed to make the home feel rustic…yet elegant.

She was wiping down the puddles on the floor by the door when Tate came into the house, worried that the water would damage the flooring.

"What the hell are you doing?" His voice was low and reverberated with what sounded like anger.

"I'm cleaning up the water on the floor. My stuff was soaked."

"Leave it."

Lara finished the job quickly and rose, but flinched at her sore thigh.

"You hurt yourself?" His voice turned to gentle concern.

"I'm okay. I hit a tree with the resort's snowmobile, though. I broke one of the skis. I'm sorry." She walked toward the laundry room to dump the towel.

"I said leave it." He took the towel from her hand, led her to the couch in the living room and motioned for her to sit. "I'll have somebody go out and get the snowmobile when the weather clears. It's no big deal."

She sat and sighed as the weight of her body was taken off her leg, allowing her thigh muscle to finally relax.

Tate went to dump the towel in the laundry room after he switched on the gas fireplace, returning in a few minutes with cups of hot chocolate and a blanket. He wrapped the blanket around her body and handed her one of the steaming mugs before he dropped onto the other end of the sofa.

"Would you mind telling me what in the hell possessed you to stay out when you knew a storm was on its way, and then to leave the damn snowmobile trail on top of that? Colorado blizzards are no joke. I talked to Chloe. She said she warned you that a storm was coming," Tate grumbled. His gray eyes surveyed her cautiously as he took a slug from his own cup.

"I-I got…lost," she lied unhappily. She didn't exactly want to deceive the man who had gone out in such a vicious storm to retrieve her, but she had no choice. "Was Chloe worried? Did she send you after me?"

He nodded and gave her an annoyed expression.

"I'm sorry. It was a stupid thing to do."

He nodded again, his gaze sharp and assessing.

Great. Now he thinks I'm an idiot, a dumb blonde who isn't smart enough to get out of an incoming blizzard. I honestly can't blame him for thinking what he's thinking right now. But I don't like it.

Strangely, she actually cared what Tate thought about her now. He'd risked his own life to come out and save her. He was irritated, and rightfully so. She kind of found herself missing his usual dimpled grin and cocky attitude. Right now, he looked dark and intense, more serious than she'd ever seen him, and that fierce expression made her squirm.

"Why did you do it? What were you really looking for, Lara? You left the trail, and I don't buy that you were totally lost." He locked eyes with her; his probing look drilled into her soul.

She opened her mouth and then closed it again, unsure of what to say to him.

I don't want to lie to him.

A small yip saved her from having to say anything as the cutest little German Shepard puppy Lara had ever seen scampered into the room, and prevented the need for her to speak.

She smiled as the tiny creature stopped at Tate's feet and wriggled around in excitement. Lara watched as he picked up the tiny canine with a gentleness that made her heart skip a beat. "Who is that?"

Tate scratched the pup's body. "This is Shep."

"Not a very unique name, Colter," she chided softly. "Is he yours?"

"He wasn't exactly planned," Tate grumbled, but he continued to scratch the puppy's quivering body. "Somebody dumped him on the highway. Probably a Christmas gift that somebody decided they didn't want chewing on their furniture. Chloe talked me into keeping him." Tate shrugged. "Hell, I figured I could take better care of him than his previous owners."

He obviously took very good care of the little ball of fur, and it was apparent to Lara that Tate already loved the pup, no matter how much he grumbled about adopting the little dog. "He looks like he's barely old enough to be weaned," she observed thoughtfully.

"Chloe says he's about ten to twelve weeks."

Lara took the puppy in her lap as Shep tumbled off Tate's thighs and crawled eagerly toward her. "He's adorable." She cuddled the pup against her breast and stroked over the silky fur as the dog licked her jaw. "How can anybody be so cruel? He could have frozen to death. He's too little and doesn't have the reserves to survive outside for long."

"He almost did freeze. He was pretty cold when I picked him up. I'm glad Chloe was around to take care of him. Getting hit by a car was fairly likely, too. The highway is pretty busy in the winter with ski traffic," Tate replied.

It was pretty hard not to like a guy who rescued puppies—and women—in distress. Tate might not be happy with her right now, but he'd saved her anyway. Lara looked up and smiled at him, and he grinned back as Shep sank his little teeth into her sweater and started to tug. She laughed merrily and disentangled the black and tan ball of fur from her garment. "He likes to chew."

"He'll be a handful," Tate agreed, not sounding the least bit daunted.

"He reminds me so much of Chief when he was a puppy. I got him for my tenth birthday. He was a Shepard, too, and his markings were similar. Chief was my constant companion for years." Lara sighed. Damn. Even now, she still missed her canine companion.

"What happened to him?" Tate asked curiously.

Shep leaped to try to investigate what was in her mug, and Lara laughed at his antics, suddenly remembering how much fun a puppy could be. "No chocolate for you, pup. It's not good for you." She held the half-empty mug higher. She looked at Tate and answered hesitantly. "I had to give him away. My parents died when I was sixteen. I had to move in with my aunt, and my uncle hated dogs." She stroked the puppy on her lap as she finished her hot chocolate and set the mug gently on a coaster on the coffee table. Her uncle had hated everything and everyone, including his wife.

"Jesus, Lara. Both of your parents died at the same time? What happened?"

Now, even a little more than thirteen years after that horrendous day, Lara had a hard time talking about her parents' death. "They were murdered."

"Tell me. How?" Tate's voice was tender and compassionate.

Lara met his eyes as she cuddled Shep for comfort. "They both died on September 11, 2001." Instinctively, she knew that Tate would make the connection and she wouldn't have to say anything more.

Tate's face turned into a look of astonishment. "They both died in the attack on the World Trade Center?"

Lara nodded slowly, her eyes moist with tears. "South Tower. They never had a chance. My dad was a lawyer. He had business in New York, and Mom went with him because their wedding anniversary was on September 12th. They wanted to celebrate in New York City. She went with him to the World Trade Center that day. Mom had told my aunt that morning that my dad just needed to make a quick stop and then he was taking her out for brunch. They were both just in the wrong place at the wrong time." How many times had Lara thought that? It wasn't like her dad had gone there every day. If only her parents had gone the day before. If only her dad wasn't such an early bird and they had planned to go later. If only...

"I'm so damn sorry, Lara," Tate rasped as he moved next to her, put his arms around her shoulders, and lowered Shep gently to the floor.

He pulled her unresisting body into his arms and cradled her head against his chest, and Lara let him. It felt so damn good to feel a human connection again, to let him comfort her, even though she shouldn't. "I still miss them." That fateful day would be forever burned into her mind.

"I know. I still miss my dad sometimes, too, even though it's getting harder and harder to remember him."

"What happened?" Lara knew Tate's father had died years ago, but she never had learned the exact cause.

"Strangely enough, he died in an act of terror, too, but it didn't happen in the US. On a trip to the Middle East in the mid-nineties, he was in the wrong place at the wrong time, just like your parents. He was killed when a car bomb exploded. It wasn't his car. He just happened to be right beside the vehicle when the bomb detonated. Terrorists claimed responsibility for it later, happy that they'd killed an American," Tate growled into her hair. "Bastards."

Lara's eyes grew wider in surprise. The coincidence that they had both lost someone dear to them in an act of terrorism was strange enough. But the fact that something like this had happened to *Marcus* was even more bizarre.

Her mind whirled as she took in all the implications of what Tate had just related. She could tell by the sorrow in Tate's voice that he still mourned his father's death. Did Marcus? If he did, things were even stranger and more puzzling than Tate could even imagine.

She clung to Tate and wrapped her arms around his neck as he rocked her gently, remorseful and nauseated at the thought that this crazy, cocky, arrogant yet kind man was going to be even more devastated when he found out the truth.

Chapter 4

Very little surprised Tate Colter anymore, but Lara's revelation earlier in the day that she'd lost her parents in the worst terrorist attack on US soil had thrown him for a loop. His family had been torn apart when they'd lost his father. He could only imagine the pain Lara must have suffered when she'd lost both of her parents at the same time. His whole family had mourned his dad for years, but they'd had his mom to keep them grounded. She'd kept their lives as normal as possible. Lara had been displaced, and lost the two people most dear to her in a shocking event that had rocked the entire country. She'd lost her home, everything normal in her life along with her parents.

"Holy shit," he whispered to himself vehemently. Those facts about her life hadn't been in the information he'd gathered on her, but then he hadn't been looking for her parentage. He'd been looking for current information about her and what she was doing in Rocky Springs.

Lara had wanted to get back to the resort, but he'd refused. Sure, he could get back to the resort if he wanted to, even though the roads were technically impassable by trucks or autos until they were plowed. Over a foot of snow had already fallen, and many areas had drifts even higher because of the high winds. And the white stuff just kept on coming. They'd be seeing several feet of new snow by the time this storm was over.

Tate had told Lara that they were stuck until the roads were plowed and he could take her safely back to the resort in his truck after the storm.

He *didn't* tell her that he had a Jeep in his extra garage with a big ass plow.

Earlier, his motivation had been clear when he'd brought her back to his place: get her into his bed so he could stop this growing pre-occupation he had with fucking her senseless. Then find out all of her secrets.

Now, he wasn't quite sure *what* his objective was exactly. Yeah, he still wanted to fuck her more than he'd ever wanted any woman in his entire life. But everything about her grew on him, drove him crazy, and sent his obsession with her into overdrive.

He turned away from his position by the picture window. *Was Lara naked right now?* She liked to eat, so she'd cooked an enormous amount of food for both of them, and they'd put away a good dinner before he showed her his personal hot springs. The muscle in her thigh was probably still sore, so he'd offered her the use of the springs. Now he wished he'd made a suggestion to share the water.

She would have refused.

"Fuck!" Tate clicked the leash on Shep's collar and walked outside. The pup looked up at him with sad brown eyes that reminded him of Lara's. Hell, just about anything reminded him of *her* right now. He crouched down and stroked the dog. "I'm not leaving you, boy. I'd just rather you didn't do your thing in the house." Tate knew the pup still had the fear of abandonment, but he wasn't going anywhere. Once he had decided to take on a responsibility, he took it seriously. What kind of asshole could dump a tiny, defenseless animal beside the road, knowing it would probably die?

The motion lights in front of the house clicked on, but it didn't help much. The blizzard still raged, and the visibility sucked. He urged the puppy toward the edge of the woods. He'd stepped out without a jacket, hoping he could cool down his heated body, and that his ever-present erection he sported whenever he thought about or saw Lara would finally deflate.

Tate was cold by the time Shep had emptied his bladder, but his dick was still hard. It was damn near impossible to clear his mind of the image of Lara lounging naked in his private mineral bath, so damn close to him that he could almost touch her.

"Let's go, buddy," he urged the puppy, pissed off at himself for getting so worked up over a woman. Shep bounced happily in front of him, eager to get back to a warm environment.

Tate kicked his boots off on the covered porch. He entered the house again and let Shep off his leash, hanging the tether on a hook next to the door. Tate patted the dog. "Good boy." He didn't know much about training a puppy, but he hoped a little praise would go a long way toward Shep not making a puddle on his floor.

Tate wandered through the house and stopped by the closed door that led to the hot springs. *Was Lara still in there? Was she taking an unordinary length of time, or did he just feel like she was because of his overactive imagination and obsession with her?*

She'd been in there for a while—since right after dinner.

"Lara," he called through the door, fairly certain she wouldn't hear him. There was a sliding door and a rock path down to the covered springs between them. He turned the handle and pushed on the door, and it sprang open.

She didn't lock the door.

Feeling both guilty and elated that she trusted him enough to leave the door unlocked, he moved soundlessly through the slider and out to the path that led to the rocky hot springs. His breath seized in his lungs as he rounded the corner.

His gaze found her immediately: she was leaned up against the wall, sitting on one of the rock seats in the spring pool, her eyes closed.

She's asleep.

He exhaled with a grunt and looked at the pile of clothing next to the pool. *She had gone in nude.* Tate didn't think, didn't debate with himself. He stripped quickly and lowered his naked body into the pool. He couldn't leave her in the springs asleep, and he didn't want to startle her. If he was honest with himself, he would probably admit that he wanted to get close to her, but he wasn't into searching his soul at the moment. Tate couldn't tear his eyes away from Lara's sleeping form, the tops of her perfect breasts revealed above the water.

She's fucking perfect.

He swept a stray lock of damp hair from her face, and examined her features, so soft and innocent in sleep. Tate ran a gentle finger across her plump, luscious lips and over the soft skin of her cheek because he just couldn't stop himself from doing it.

He'd had plenty of women in his life. Sure, none of his relationships had been very intense, and they were quickly over because of his past career in Special Forces. Yeah, he'd been going through a period of disinterest since his accident, but that was understandable. Thinking back, his ennui had really started even before he'd gotten injured, and it had continued until the day he met Lara. It was as if his dick had gone from zero to full throttle in a matter of seconds. Why in the hell was he so drawn to *this* particular woman, a female who could kick ass herself, and probably had no need for the overactive protective instincts that emanated from him every time he looked at her?

He hurt for the pain she'd suffered from losing her parents so young, and then wanted to hurt the guy who had cheated on her. She acted so tough. Actually, she *was* a strong woman, but there was an underlying softness in Lara that he wanted to reach, needed to touch. He liked her rough edges and her tough exterior, but he wanted her submission, and he wanted her to surrender to him and only to him.

"Wake up, sweetheart," he whispered roughly in her ear.

She stirred and wrapped her arms around his neck. "Tate." She sighed softly.

The sound of his name on her lips nearly gutted him completely. Her soft capitulation made his cock harder than it had ever been before. "Wake up, baby." He wasn't going to take advantage of her sleepy state. Not that he didn't want to use her vulnerable state to steal a taste of her lips...but his damn conscience wouldn't let him.

"I am awake now," she murmured sensually. She pulled his head down and his lips to hers.

Hell, there was only so much a guy could take, and Tate had reached his limit. His need was reigning supreme.

He captured her lips like a starving man attacked a feast, losing the battle with his conscience while his treacherous mind and body had their own damn celebration.

Lara's sleepy brain knew exactly who was kissing her, and she opened to Tate like a flower seeking the sunlight. He conquered and cajoled, teased and subdued, plundered her mouth as though he owned it. Lara moaned against his lips; her tongue dueled with his for dominance. She lost, and she reveled in defeat, letting this man who made her feel like a woman command her. He made the rules and she happily followed, intoxicated with not having to think, to just respond. Although he dominated, she'd never felt safer than she did right now, or more desired and wanted.

He lifted her, finally releasing her mouth as he carried her up the stone steps and into the house. After he lowered her feet slowly to the ground in the bathroom attached to the large bedroom they had entered, Tate turned on the shower with a flick of his strong wrist.

"We need to rinse off," he said huskily.

The pungent smell of the minerals in the water still clung to her wet skin, and she stepped into the warm water willingly. As she dunked her head under the shower head, she let the pulsating, streaming liquid relax her already limp body even more.

Tate stepped in behind her, lathered shampoo onto her scalp and rubbed it in, massaging the soap into her hair.

Oh, God, he feels good.

Lara let her body relax against his powerful chest and abdomen, not questioning *why* she trusted Tate. It felt right, and she just did. Maybe it should feel awkward to be leaning against a naked man in a shower, a guy who she hardly knew, especially when she was as bare as the day she was born herself. But the closeness and the physical intimacy just made her yearn for an even deeper connection with Tate, a bond that she'd never felt before.

"Are you okay?" he rasped roughly in her ear.

"I-I'm fine. I'm sorry I fell asleep."

"Don't be sorry, Lara. I was here. You knew you were safe," he told her in a low, sexy baritone. "How's your leg?"

She didn't speak for a moment as he gently tilted her head down and rinsed her hair.

"It's better," she told him tremulously as he smoothly switched their positions so he could rinse soap from his hair. The hot springs had soothed the muscle in her thigh, and the pain was dull and almost nonexistent now.

He soaped up his body, and then refilled his palm with the liquid, smoothing it over her shoulders and back. "You're so damn beautiful, Lara." His voice was hoarse and graveled.

She shuddered as his slick hands moved around her torso and slid up to palm her breasts. "Tate," she whispered. Her head fell back against his shoulder.

"That's right, baby. Keep on saying my name. Moan my name while you come. Know exactly who is making you feel like this," he demanded as his thumbs circled her sensitive nipples.

Her core clenched almost viciously as Tate lightly pinched the hardened peaks of her breasts, and set her body on fire with desperate need. "Please, Tate," she whimpered. His hard erection was right against her lower back. "I need...I need..."

"I know what you need," he answered gruffly. His hand slid down her belly and into the trimmed hair at her mound. "You need to get off. And I'm going to get you there," he growled into her ear.

"Yes." She breathed a tortured sigh of relief as his fingers delved between her thighs while his other hand continued to tease her nipples relentlessly.

"Jesus. You're so fucking wet for me, Lara. So hot and tight." He probed her sheath with his index finger. "Are you so slick because you want my cock inside you?"

"Oh, God, yes." Lara wanted Tate more than she had ever wanted a man in her entire life. She'd been dreaming about him in the pool, about this, before he'd woken her up. Now, she wasn't quite sure where the dream had ended and the reality began. All she knew now was that he was hot, hard, and she needed him. "Fuck me, Tate. Please."

He pinched her nipple a little harder and demanding fingers sought and found her clit. He stroked over the pulsating bundle of nerves roughly. "Do you know what it does to me to hear you begging me to fuck you? It makes me want to give you exactly what you want."

Lara moaned as her slick body slid against his muscular form, and she arched her back as he worked her clit harder with his thumb and index finger. "Oh, Jesus. I can't take anymore," she screamed. The coil in her belly started to unfurl.

"You can. Take it, Lara. Use it to come for me, baby," he commanded harshly in her ear.

His husky, lust-filled voice made her body quiver and as his mouth moved to her neck, lightly nipping and lapping at the sensitive skin, Lara completely shattered. "Tate!" The ripples in her channel became massive spasms. Her climax gripped her hard and refused to let go.

"Need to feel you coming," Tate growled.

Instinctively, she knew exactly what he wanted. Lara turned blindly, wrapped her arms around his neck and jumped, locking her legs around his waist. "Then feel it now," she panted heavily. "Right now."

"Fuck. Lara. I wasn't going to—"

Knowing now that he loved to hear her beg, she pleaded, "Fuck me, Tate. I need your cock inside me now. No more waiting." Lara needed him to lose control completely.

She looked up at him; the strain showed in his tortured expression. Their gazes locked, and she stared down at Tate's ferocious desire firing in his eyes. "I want you." She reached down between them to grip his massive shaft and fit the head against the entrance to her sheath.

"Oh, fuck yeah. Mine," he growled as he pinned her against the wall of the shower and buried himself to his balls.

Lara gasped, but her eyes never left Tate's. Her climax had ended, the muscles of her channel relaxed to allow the invasion of his massive cock, and clenched around him like a glove. His fingers bit into her ass as he held her tightly against his groin. She speared her fingers into his wet hair. "Fuck me—"

"Don't say it again, Lara, or you're going to get more than you bargained for," Tate said in a dangerous, out-of-control rasp.

His eyes were wild and carnal, and Lara reveled in them. "Fuck me," she said deliberately. "Please fuck me." She wasn't afraid of this man's fierceness. It made her hotter than she'd ever been before, and an answering urgency came from deep inside her to push him to the limit.

Something between a growl and a groan left his mouth before it crashed down on hers. His hips moved in a punishing rhythm as his cock pummeled into her.

Tate fucked her mouth with his tongue the same way he did with his cock: hot, hard, feral and earthy, at a pace so fast that Lara could hardly keep up. She just held onto him and enjoyed the ride.

He tore his mouth from hers, resting his forehead against the shower wall as his chest rose and fell heavily. He ground his hips against her pussy with every thrust, lifting her higher and closer to another, more explosive release. "Feels so good," she gasped.

"Too damn good," Tate answered in a passion-laden grunt. "Need. To. Make. You. Come. Before. Me."

Every thrust drove her higher, and there was no question she would tip over the edge. But Tate sounded desperate, driven. She didn't want him to hold back anymore. Taking one of her hands from his hair, she reached between their bodies with her fingers and stroked over her clit. With a sharply drawn breath, she sent herself careening into space; her sheath clamped down on his cock as he entered and retreated.

"Fuck, baby," he groaned. His big body shuddered against hers.

Lara screamed as her orgasm ripped through her body. Her internal walls squeezed and released Tate as he found his own release. He buried himself deep inside her one last time with a tormented groan.

He held her body tightly against him. Tate sat down on a marble seat in the massive shower and clutched her body as though he never wanted to let her go. He closed his mouth over hers, kissing her sensually, gently, before he released her lips and rested his forehead on her shoulder. "You nearly killed me," he panted harshly.

"Are you complaining?" she teased breathlessly.

"Christ, no. It would be a hell of a way to go." He leaned back and shot her a very naughty, dimpled grin.

Chapter 5

The next morning, Lara eased out of the huge bed—presumably Tate's—and sprinted to the closet to search for some clothing. She grabbed a tan robe from its hanger, slipped it on, and hustled out to the kitchen, her mind whirling.

What the hell was I thinking?

In reality, she hadn't been thinking at all. She'd reacted. Falling into a twilight sleep, she'd been in the midst of an erotic dream fantasy about Tate when she'd heard his voice next to her in the pool. Wanting for her dream to become reality, she'd made it come true. Once he'd kissed her, she'd been doomed. Tate Colter was every woman's fantasy, and she was far from immune to him. She'd fought her strange connection and attraction to him since he'd first smiled at her, resisted the temptation to kiss that sexy indentation on his cheek the minute she saw it.

Lara smiled down at Shep as the little fur ball danced at her feet. "You need to pee, huh?" As she looked around, she was amazed there wasn't already a puddle on the floor somewhere.

"I'll take him out," Tate said in a sensual voice graveled with sleep from behind Lara.

Startled by his presence, Lara whirled around and caught his eyes roving over the silk robe that clung to her body. "I borrowed it. Sorry."

His lips turned up sensually. "Don't be sorry. It looks sexy as hell on you, and I don't use it."

He was already dressed in a pair of jeans and a sweatshirt, his feet bare. "Let's go, buddy, before you do your thing on the floor." Tate opened the front door and pulled on his boots.

Before Tate could catch him, Shep's little body flew out the door from behind him.

"Oh, no," Lara groaned.

"He won't go far. I guess he had to go pretty bad," Tate remarked, his voice amused.

"It's freezing." Lara pulled the robe tighter around her body as she leaned against the doorjamb and watched the puppy as he ventured out toward the edge of the woods. "Don't you want a jacket?"

"Worried about me?" Tate straightened after he pulled on his boots, sounding as if he liked the thought of her fretting over him. He crowded her up against the door frame and trapped her with one hand on the outside wall and one on the inside. "I woke up with my dick already hard, and the sight of that sweet bare ass of yours walking to the closet. I think I need to get just a little bit cold right now." His eyes caressed her face as though he searched for something.

"Okay." She almost blushed like a teenager. *Dammit.* Tate Colter got to her with the simplest of statements, rendering her senseless. Last night had proved that with a vengeance.

As he dropped his arms and turned around to follow Shep, Lara took a deep breath.

Get it together, Lara. It's bad enough that you begged the man to fuck you last night. You need to pull your shit back together again. You have a mission to accomplish, and being involved with Tate Colter is trouble.

Disgusted with herself, Lara started to close the door, but she caught a sudden movement out of the corner of her eye. She opened the door again, oblivious now to the bitter cold wind. Her brows narrowed as she realized that it wasn't a larger dog that stalked the puppy, moving slowly closer to the defenseless little ball of fur. It was a large coyote.

"Tate!" she shouted, putting urgency in her voice as the coyote moved closer, no more than thirty or forty feet now from the tiny Shep.

"I see him," Tate called back, his eyes focused on the predator. He reached down to the ground, digging underneath the snow. He picked up some rocks and sticks and flung them with accuracy toward the hungry coyote. The animal yelped from a direct hit with a small rock, but didn't run away like a coyote usually would when hazed by a human. Tate cursed at the animal, yelled, and continued to toss anything he could find at the stalking predator, but the coyote just let out a low, feral growl.

Lara could see the ribs on the wild canine, and it was skinny, obviously hungry enough to feed on anything. "You're not making Tate's innocent puppy your damn breakfast," Lara muttered angrily. She ran into the bedroom where she had shed her clothing the night before and was back to the door in seconds.

Stepping outside just in time to see Tate lunge for the puppy at the same time the coyote went in for the kill, she lifted her arms as Tate sprinted toward the door with his pet in his arms. The coyote turned to give chase with an angry howl.

The coyote would be on Tate in moments unless...

Given no choice, Lara sighted and shot the pursuing predator right between the eyes.

She lowered her arms slowly; the Glock 23 pistol came to rest against her thigh as she let out a sigh of relief. She had no doubt that the coyote was after the puppy. They rarely attacked humans. But if Tate got in the way, he could be torn up or even killed. She wasn't about to let either the puppy or Tate get injured if she could help it.

But she'd need to think fast to explain.

"That was one hell of a shot," Tate rumbled as he jogged up to the porch. Shep whined in his arms. He dropped the puppy inside the door and Shep scampered into the house gladly. "I'm not sure if it was the coyote or the gunshot that scared the piss right out of him," Tate drawled as he watched Shep run for cover inside the house, seemingly totally unfazed by the fact that he could have gotten injured.

"I'm sorry. I didn't have a choice. The coyote was giving chase and you weren't going to make it to the house," Lara argued defensively.

Tate wandered over to the dead animal and then back to Lara, nudging her to get back inside the house. "You don't have any shoes on. Get back inside."

She went back into the house and set her Glock gently on a high kitchen cupboard to prevent Shep from getting near it. "I really didn't have any other option," Lara told Tate again as she turned to him when she felt his presence behind her.

"Hey." He dropped his hands on her shoulders. "I'm not arguing. Your quick actions and fucking awesome sharpshooting probably saved me some injuries and Shep's life. Some of the coyotes are getting bold. I'm not sure if that one was rabid, but I know it was hungry. The tourists think it's fun to leave food out so they can see them, and then they lose their natural fear of humans, become habituated. He definitely wanted to make Shep a meal. I'm not mad at you. I'm grateful."

"You are?" Lara looked at Tate, confused.

He nodded. "You're a damn good shot. And you carry a gun. Why?"

They were the questions Lara wanted to avoid. "Because I—I'm..."

Tate covered her lips with his fingers. "Don't lie to me. I know you want to, or you feel you need to, but don't. You don't need to." His brows drew together as he studied her carefully. "You're Special Agent Lara Bailey from the FBI. You're assigned to the counter-terrorism division, which makes a lot of sense to me now that I know how you lost your parents. My question isn't *who* you are, Lara. My question is what in the hell are you doing *here* in Rocky Springs, Colorado?"

She stepped back until his hands fell from her body, completely in shock that her status as an agent had been discovered so easily. "How did you know?" She wasn't going to deny it. There was obviously no point.

He smirked knowingly. "I've got connections you wouldn't believe. All it took was a phone call. What I couldn't discover was your mission. You aren't a stressed-out employee on vacation. You're here for reason."

She folded her arms in front of her. "How do you know that? Being a field agent is a stressful job. And we do get vacation." Lara just couldn't remember ever taking one. She took a deep breath before she continued. "And how is it possible for you to find out my status that easily? I know that you were a Navy SEAL, but it wasn't on your military records. Why? And how is it that you still have such powerful contacts?"

Tate folded his arms in front of him and mimicked her stance. "Maybe I wasn't a SEAL," he suggested calmly. "If it's not in my records, it didn't happen."

"Bullshit." She glared back at him. "You went through BUD/s training, SQT and you got your SEAL Trident. After that, it's like you disappeared, except for the notations that you were a Special Forces officer with an exemplary record. You left because you were injured in the line of duty, but the mission was highly classified. What kind of mission is classified for an FBI agent?"

"The kind that doesn't exist to almost anybody in the government," he explained casually. "And I never claimed to be a SEAL. Although I'll admit that I let anyone who thought so continue to assume that I was. I didn't have a choice."

Lara gaped at him. "You were in a top-secret Special Forces team? They recruited you from the SEAL team, didn't they?"

She'd heard occasional rumors about a kick-ass special operations team that was known to almost no one, even the upper echelon of the FBI. But she'd blown off the continual rumors. His military record made sense to her. It was the only thing that did make sense. If he'd continued on as a Navy SEAL, his record would have reflected it. SEALs weren't hidden from the FBI. None of the known Special Forces were hidden from the FBI. The only answer was a top-secret team, a team so elite that nobody knew about them except the very top of the food chain in the government. She'd never seen a military file like Tate's, but it made perfect sense now.

She raised her brow when he didn't answer, and he just shrugged. "I'd rather hear about you, Special Agent Bailey. Like what in the hell are you doing here? And don't try to feed me the vacation bullshit. It won't fly. The only thing I haven't been able to put together is why you're here when you're a counter-terrorist agent. Is there a terrorist hiding out way out here in Rocky Springs?"

"It's possible," she hedged.

"Who?"

"I can't give you that information, Colter. You of all people should understand keeping secrets."

Tate moved forward and pinned her body against the kitchen cupboard. "Not from me. I grew up here. I live here. And I'm damn sure I have a higher security clearance than you do. You have no reason *not* to tell me. This is my turf. My brother is a goddamn US Senator. What if he's a target?" he growled. The fierceness in his eyes glared at her terrifyingly.

"He's not," she told him sharply. She could share that much. The last thing she wanted was for him to think his brother Blake was in danger. "And if you're out of the military, you no longer have clearance."

Tate looked at her, and spoke as though he picked his words carefully. "I still do. We'll just say I'm a consultant of sorts now."

"To who?" There wasn't a damn thing in his background check to indicate that, but there was never a file like his either. For some reason, most information on Tate Colter was hidden, buried beneath superficial bullshit.

He shrugged.

"Are you still military? What kind of accident did you have?"

He stared at her with an innocent expression. "I broke my leg in a skiing accident."

Lara rolled her eyes. "Sure you did. The accident is in your file, Colter. It happened while you were on active duty. You left the military because of it. It just doesn't say what happened."

"Nobody in my family knows that. I told them all that it happened while I was away skiing in Vail. As far as my family is concerned, it's not job related. I left Colorado as soon as I had my last surgery just to get away. I found a place in Florida, hung out with a friend there so I didn't have to keep lying to my family. I didn't come back here until I was completely healed."

"I won't tell."

"It was the result of a helicopter crash. I was the pilot. If I wasn't flying it, I'd be dead. We all made it out. But I had to have corrective surgery, pins to put my leg back together," he said slowly, cautiously.

"Nobody would ever know. You don't limp."

Tate shook his head. "*I* knew. It made me slower. Being slower means getting dead, and possibly causing other members of a team to get hurt or dead, too."

Holy shit. If Tate Colter was slow now, he would have made her head spin before his accident. "So you gave up your position in Special Forces."

"I had to. I knew I wasn't in perfect physical condition." His voice sounded pained to admit that he wasn't flawless.

"Did that hurt? To admit you're human?" she asked him quietly. Special Forces were cocky for a reason. If they didn't have ultimate faith in their ability to do anything, accomplish any mission, they could very well die if they doubted their abilities. Obviously Tate was able to assess his situation and step down. She admired that ability, and she wasn't mocking him.

"Damn right it hurt," he grumbled. "But I don't want anybody killed because I couldn't admit that I wasn't the same as I was before the...accident."

Lara had a suspicion that the helicopter hadn't just crashed. It had probably been shot down. But she didn't bother to ask because he obviously wasn't going to share the experience. If he'd been involved in some type of top-secret black ops team, he wasn't going to talk to a virtual stranger about it, even if she was FBI.

We aren't exactly strangers. We were intimate. Okay...maybe not intimate...maybe I was just a lay for him.

He'd treated her as if she was special, and try as she may, she couldn't get last night out of her head. He'd dried her off like a treasured woman after they'd left the shower, brushed out her hair, and scooped her up and taken her to bed. She'd been out almost as soon as her head hit the pillow, falling asleep with Tate's body sheltering her protectively.

"I'm sorry I didn't tell you," she murmured, seeing a quick flash of vulnerability in his eyes.

"I had no problem finding out. And I wasn't angry. You're an agent. That's not something you go around telling everyone. I know what it's like to need to hide certain parts of your life." He paused for a moment and speared his fingers through her hair. He tilted her head up and searched her face before he added, "It's lonely."

She nodded slowly, not looking away from him. "It can be. I don't have many real friends because I live for my job. I'm pretty much on the job twenty-four hours a day, seven days a week. It doesn't leave much time for socializing."

"And the asshole who cheated on you?"

"It happened two years ago. He was an agent, too, in a different department, thank God. I don't have to see him every day. It was convenient. We both worked long hours, got together when we could. But I thought we were monogamous. He didn't. It hurt, but it didn't break me." She tried to look away, but he turned her head up again to keep eye contact.

"Who have you been with since then?" His voice was demanding.

"Nobody until you," she admitted. "I know we didn't use a condom last night. It was careless of both of us. But I'm clean, and I'm still on birth control—"

"I know you're clean. I saw your last physical. I knew you were on birth control, too. It was in your medical records."

"You looked at my damn medical records," she said irritably. Really, what the hell else did he have access to?

"You saw mine," he reminded her cheekily. "Fair is fair. And if you didn't see a physical, I'm completely free of any diseases. I never fuck without a condom. And I haven't been with anybody at all since my accident."

Lara gasped softly. "Why?" She would have thought that Tate Colter would have a ton of women waiting in line to jump into his bed.

"Because there was nobody I wanted to be with, Lara. My leg isn't a pretty sight, and the desire just wasn't there," he answered bluntly. "Before that I lived for my job, too."

"What changed?" She held her breath. His eyes drilled into hers, smoky and possessive as he stared.

"I saw you." He stroked an errant lock of hair from her cheek. "My dick has been hard ever since," he said unhappily.

Lara laughed until she snorted.

"It's not funny," Tate growled, annoyed.

"I'm not exactly a femme fatale." Just the idea made her want to laugh again. "I eat like a pig. I hate dressing in heels, and I rarely bother to put on makeup unless I'm forced to. I don't bother messing with my hair, and I'm most comfortable in jeans or a dark pantsuit and ugly, comfortable, flat shoes for work. I work in a male-dominated field, so I have to be tough. Most of the time I'd rather be kicking a guy's ass than screwing him. How is that the least bit sexy?" She pushed on his chest and stepped away from him to put a safe distance between them.

He leaned a jean-clad hip against the kitchen counter and grinned at her. "There's something really erotic about a woman with a gun who wants to attack me."

"You're deranged." She covered her mouth to stifle a laugh. Dammit! He was so freaking hot that she *did* want to jump him. There was no denying they were attracted to each other. Sparks were almost visible as the heat and chemistry flowed between the two of them, making it very hard for her to keep her hands to herself.

One of the most attractive things about Tate—and there were unfortunately way too many of those—was that he accepted her exactly the way she was. He found her desirable even though she rarely released the feminine side of herself. Not only was he attracted to her, but he also seemed to actually *like* her.

He stepped toward her again. "I already told you that a woman with a healthy appetite turns me on."

She stepped back out of his dangerous reach. "That reminds me that I'm starving." Actually, her heart flip-flopped around in her chest. Every trait of hers that he mentioned that he accepted as sexy made her just a little bit giddy. "I was going to make breakfast. Now that the weather is clear, I need to get going after breakfast."

His face turned grim. "You have to tell me what's going on, Lara. I can help. If you don't tell me, I'll tail you. So you might as well spill it. I know you were headed toward Marcus's property when you had your accident on the sled. Were you trying to get his cooperation in an investigation?"

Her heart clenched, and she hesitated. She *shouldn't* tell him anything, but he had a *right* to know, and he might be able to help. However, she didn't want to hurt him. "No. I wasn't trying to get his cooperation."

He gave her a questioning look. "Then what were you doing?"

She sighed. "Your brother Marcus is actually a suspect. We have very good reason to believe that your brother is instrumental in trying to organize a large-scale terrorist attack. I was sent here to investigate your oldest brother, Tate. I'm so sorry."

He didn't react at all like Lara expected. Tate Colter did the one thing it never even occurred to her that he might do when he found out about Marcus.

He laughed.

Chapter 6

"Did you and Dad ever fight?" Chloe Colter asked her mother as they sat at the table together to have a late breakfast. Her mom had arrived home on an early-morning flight, and Chloe had gone out to the airstrip to pick her up.

Aileen Colter loved every one of her children equally, and worried about different problems with each one of them. But right now, she was concerned about Chloe. Her only daughter and youngest child had always had the sunniest personality, a happiness that always seemed to radiate from her being. Lately, that bright light that was her Chloe seemed to have disappeared. "Sometimes we did," she answered her daughter carefully, wondering why Chloe asked about her relationship with her husband, Chloe's father.

Chloe put down her fork, her food untouched, and reached for her coffee. "I never remember hearing you two argue."

Aileen looked at Chloe's full plate and frowned. "What happened to your wrist?" When her daughter had put her fork down, she'd noticed bruises on her arm.

"James was trying to teach me some martial arts moves. It was an accident," Chloe explained.

An accident? Maybe it had been accidental, but how had James bruised up Chloe's arm by teaching her beginner martial arts? It wasn't a tiny bruise. Her entire wrist and arm was purple and yellow. "Your father and I did disagree sometimes, but we respected each other enough not to yell." Her deceased husband, Russell Colter, *had* been a handful—just like his boys—but he'd never raised his voice. He had never had to. Aileen had always sensed when something was wrong, and they'd been able to talk it out. If things got out of hand and they wanted to vent, they never did it around the children, and they never disrespected each other.

"He had a lot of responsibility," Chloe mused. "Did he never get angry and take it out on you?"

"Never," Aileen told her daughter emphatically. "He talked to me about it, but he never blamed me for anything that wasn't my fault." She studied her daughter's face, and noted the dark circles under Chloe's eyes and the stress lines around her mouth. "Is everything all right between you and James, sweetheart?"

"Yeah. Fine. They're fine," Chloe answered quickly. Maybe too quickly. "He just seems pre-occupied and stressed out about work. And with me starting my practice, things are a little tense, I guess."

Something *was* wrong. Aileen could sense it. But her daughter was an adult, nearly thirty years old, and she was so proud of Chloe. She didn't want to pry, but she planned to watch their relationship much closer. Her instincts as a mother were rarely wrong. "You know you can talk to me about anything?"

Chloe smiled at her weakly. "I know, Mom. Thanks. I missed you while you were gone."

Aileen had missed her children, too. Chloe had been gone for school for so long, and now she was getting married and leaving home for good in a matter of months. Luckily, James was a local doctor and they would live here in Rocky Springs, but she'd gotten used to having Chloe back in the house again, and it would be hard to see her move out again.

I wish I could get rid of this nagging, motherly feeling that something isn't right with Chloe. I'm sure it's just because I'm sad that she's leaving. James is a doctor, a respected physician, and my daughter is a local veterinarian now. He and Chloe should live a wonderful life together.

Unfortunately, Chloe just didn't seem like a happy bride-to-be, and James was polite but distant. He always had been, so it was difficult to really get to know him well. "You and James haven't gotten your rings yet?" Aileen knew her daughter wanted a ring. She'd seen Chloe look longingly at wedding bands and diamonds for months. Ultimately, she knew that Chloe wanted a child. Although her daughter had plenty of time left to have babies, Aileen wondered whether Chloe felt as though her biological clock was already ticking. There were moments where she wondered whether Chloe wanted a child more than she really wanted a husband.

"He still wants to wait until closer to the wedding."

A male voice behind Aileen startled her.

"Then dump the loser and marry me instead."

Aileen smiled and turned around, happy to see her son, Blake, and his friend Gabriel Walker, the mysterious male voice teasing her daughter.

"Blake," Aileen said excitedly as she jumped out of her chair quickly for a woman her age and threw herself at her son.

Blake's duties as a US Senator had kept him in Washington DC for way too long. He hadn't been back to Rocky Springs in months.

He picked her up and swung her around. "How's my favorite mother?" Blake joked as he hugged her tightly.

She swatted Blake's shoulder. "I'm your *only* mother. Now put me down." She scolded him, but she secretly adored the way her children were able to openly display their affections for her and for one another. They fought and scrapped like all siblings did, but their devotion to one another was always evident. And she was so blessed with the children she and Russell had created together: every one of her kids a child to be proud of, and that she loved with all of her heart.

He squeezed her tightly before he lowered her feet back to the ground. "Ah…well…even if I had fifty mothers, you'd still be my favorite," Blake answered glibly.

Sweet talker! Of all of her boys, Blake was the most charming—which was probably good because he was a politician. But honestly, Blake had always been that way. Even as a child, he could charm the rattles off a rattlesnake.

Gabriel held out his arms to her, and Aileen didn't hesitate to hug him. "It's so good to see you, Gabe." It was *always* nice to see Gabe Walker. He and Blake had been friends since they were teens, and Gabe was living permanently in Rocky Springs now. He owned a very profitable horse ranch that bordered Blake's cattle ranch, which stretched way beyond the city limits of Rocky Springs. Her husband and Gabe's father had been good friends, and Blake and Gabe had bonded like brothers when they were teens. Aileen had also been friends with Gabe's mom, and she'd hurt for him when he lost first his mother, and then his father. Since then, she looked at him almost like another son. He had to be lonely all by himself out in the big mansion he'd built on his horse property, but he never spoke about it.

Gabe had obviously known Blake was coming in. He'd probably met him out at the airstrip and followed him home for breakfast.

As she released Gabe, Aileen turned to her daughter, who had risen to throw herself at her brother, Blake. Her second eldest son was currently nearly squeezing the life out of his little sister.

Aileen asked her daughter jokingly, "You just got another marriage proposal, darling. Aren't you going to respond to Gabe's offer?"

"No," Chloe answered irritably as she glared at Gabe. "I'm already spoken for."

Aileen had to bite her lip to keep from smiling. The way that Chloe and Gabe sparred amused her. Secretly, she wished that her Chloe *was* marrying a man like Gabe. He'd keep her on her toes without bringing her down. Gabe was obviously fond of Chloe, but her daughter was having none of him. For some reason, Chloe avoided Gabe at every opportunity.

Gabe caught Chloe's gaze and winked at her. "You know you were just waiting for a better offer to come along."

"Then I'd have to wait forever," Chloe told him in almost a hostile voice, but she shot him a fake smile. "Luckily I'm marrying the man of my dreams in just a few more months."

"If you were my woman, I'd have a ring on that finger by now." Gabe's voice was light, but his eyes were intense.

"It's a good thing I'm not your woman then," Chloe answered sharply.

Blake spoke up to dispel the tension in the room. "Where is everybody?"

"Zane's in Denver, working on a project. Marcus was due home yesterday, but he got delayed by the storm. He should be home today. And Tate is at home." Aileen motioned for everybody to sit down and she went and dished up some breakfast for the two men. She didn't miss the fact that Chloe was quick to pull her long-sleeved shirt all the way down to cover her bruised wrist.

"I think Tate has a thing for a woman who is staying here at the resort. I went to see if Lara was in the gym this morning and she wasn't there. I think she might have ended up being stranded with Tate," Chloe told Blake excitedly. She sat back in her chair, with Blake seated on her right and Gabe to her left. She ignored Gabe completely.

Blake's eyes widened. "Oh? And who is this mystery woman, and why would she be stranded with my little brother?"

Chloe relayed what she knew about Lara, and how she hadn't come back from snowmobiling yesterday before the storm. And then she proceeded to explain that Tate had gone out to look for Lara. "He texted me that he found her and told me she was safe, but she never came back to the resort last night. She has to be with him. I like her. She kicked James's rear at judo."

"Mr. Black Belt?" Gabe interjected sarcastically.

Without looking at Gabe, Chloe answered him defensively, "James is really good, but Lara is fantastic. She offered to teach me some of her self-defense moves."

"So you think this Lara is still at Tate's place?" Blake asked.

"She has to be. Maybe it was closer. The blizzard was pretty bad yesterday," Chloe told her brother thoughtfully.

"And Tate has a Jeep with a plow that could have easily brought her back to the resort," Blake reminded Chloe with a massive grin on his face.

Aileen put a heaping plate of eggs, bacon, and toast in front of Blake and Gabe. "Eat. And don't tease your brother about liking a woman. He's had a difficult year. It would be nice if at least one of my boys were thinking about marriage and grandchildren."

Tate had transitioned out of the military Special Forces, a fact that had delighted Aileen to no end. She'd gotten tired of worrying about her youngest son putting himself in harm's way every single day. But she knew he missed it, and that he was restless. A good woman might go a long way to helping her youngest boy become more content.

Tate had healed from his injury that had caused him to leave the military, an injury that he insisted had happened when he was skiing while he was off duty. *Humph!* Did her youngest son really think she bought *that* excuse? She knew he was trying to save her some worry, but she hadn't bought that lame story for a minute. A mother just…knows.

"Mom, I'm a United States Senator. Do you really think I'd be immature enough to give Tate a hard time over a woman?" Blake protested before he dug into his plate of food.

"Yes."

"Yes."

Chloe and Gabe both answered emphatically at the same time.

Aileen sat down with her coffee, happy as she watched Gabe and Chloe look at each other in surprise and exchange a small smile for the very first time.

Lara hated putting on dirty clothing, but she figured she could change when she got back to the resort. Her clothing in place, she adjusted her concealed Glock 23 at her back and lowered her sweater over the top.

"What are you doing?" Tate wandered into the bedroom.

"I'm getting ready to go back to the resort," she told him in a clipped tone, still pissed off at him because he hadn't stopped laughing since she revealed that she was investigating Marcus. She guessed he'd recovered, because he wasn't laughing now. She'd finally stomped out of the kitchen when he'd been laughing nonstop for five freaking minutes.

"So you can investigate an innocent man?" Tate's voice still held a hint of humor.

She turned around and crossed her arms in front of her. "I'm tired, I'm hungry, and I'm armed. Don't screw with me, Colter."

"Damn, you're hot when you're pissed off." He shot her an amorous look.

"Don't even think about it." She held out her arm as he advanced, walked around him and stomped back into the kitchen. She felt his presence behind her. "I have a job to do, and I don't appreciate you making fun of what I do."

"Hey." He caught her arm in the kitchen and swung her around. "I'm not making fun of what you do. You have an important and dangerous job, and you're obviously good at it. But you're hunting the wrong guy."

"The wrong guy who has been bringing in enough explosives to blow up an entire state? The wrong guy who has been dealing with known terrorists? The wrong guy who is storing weapons of mass destruction somewhere on this acreage in Rocky Springs? You mean *that* wrong guy?" she asked furiously.

Tate gaped at her. "That's not possible. Marcus is a straight arrow, Lara, and as ethical as they come. I'd tell you if I thought differently, but he doesn't have it in him to do that, and you already know what happened to my dad. Marcus loved him, and he suffered the most when Dad died because he was the eldest and the closest to our father. Christ! The last thing Marcus would do would be seen anywhere near a damn terrorist, much less be part of a plot to blow up innocent people."

Lara's heart sank. How could she convince a man who loved his brother that his sibling was really a terrorist disguised as a businessman? "We have proof, Tate. I wouldn't be here if we didn't. The FBI isn't going to waste money on an investigation without just cause. I'm sorry."

"Show me your proof. I'll help you. Where is this supposed stash?" Tate asked impatiently.

"That we don't know. That's why I'm here," Lara admitted. "All we know is that Marcus has been buying enough explosives to blow up a very large area and transporting it here. He's been seen with known terrorists. The members of this group are pretty powerful, wealthy, and well disguised as businessmen. Most of them live here in the US right now, Middle Eastern emigrants."

"Marcus would want to kill every one of them if he knew they were members of a terrorist group." Tate paced the kitchen. "He doesn't have the storage for that kind of equipment at his house."

"He built an airstrip in the summer—"

"So we could all land our jets here instead of in Denver. We all wanted it."

"He also built a new hangar."

"His other one is smaller and it was getting old. He has a brand new jet. But I'll take you to the airstrip to check it out if it will satisfy you that he's innocent. In the meantime, I'd like to hear about all of your supposed evidence against Marcus," Tate demanded. He turned his intense gaze on her.

Lara looked into his eyes, trying to read his intentions. He could be a huge help or a hindrance.

"You either trust me or you don't, baby. Make the choice," Tate growled.

"Done. I have the files on my laptop at the resort." She'd made her decision. Her gut trusted Tate. Even if Marcus *was* his brother, he wasn't going to allow him to kill innocent people. He'd spent years of his life trying to stop that very thing from happening.

"We'll check out the hangars and the airstrip first. I need five minutes to take a shower and change."

"I'll make some breakfast," Lara agreed. "We have to eat." The investigation had taken this long; it could wait another hour.

"Lara?" Tate called her name as she headed for the kitchen.

"Yeah?" She turned back to him.

"I'd trust Marcus with my life. We're going to find out this is all one big misunderstanding," he told her huskily.

She nodded. Her heart wrenched for him. "I hope we do, Tate. I really do."

He turned and strode to the bathroom without another word.

Chapter 7

"Why did you fuck me last night? Was it because you wanted to, or because you wanted information?" Tate asked Lara casually.

She glanced at him. The questioning and slightly vulnerable look in his eyes belied his nonchalant question. They had come back to the resort so she could change clothing and grab her extra gun, a compact Glock 27 that she was currently strapping to her ankle with her foot propped up on the bed.

"Regardless of what you might think, I don't screw people for information," she told him defensively as she pulled the denim of her jeans over the compact gun. "I wanted you. It's actually not a good thing to get involved with a suspect's family in any intimate way, and I shouldn't have done it as a federal officer on a case, but I haven't wanted to be with anybody in so long."

"So you were just hot for my body? You couldn't resist me?" he asked with a boyish grin. He looked up at her from his supine position on her bed, his hands behind his head as he watched her.

Lara actually felt her face turn red. *Cocky, obnoxious man!* He drove her crazy. One moment he looked so unguarded, and the next he spewed comments like the one that had just come out of his mouth. "Don't flatter yourself, Colter. I've been having a dry spell."

"Hey, I'm not complaining. I'd be more than happy to make your dry spell wet again. Feel free to use me to get you wet any time you want," he shot back at her with an innocent expression.

You already make me wet!

Tate Colter was far from angelic, even if he might look that way occasionally. She studied him. Her core flooded with heat as she openly stared at his ripped body. He was dressed in a pair of faded jeans that hugged his body like a lover, and an old T-shirt that matched his eyes. She could see every defined muscle of his abdomen and chest through the thin material, and his biceps flexed as they stretched to accommodate the position of his hands behind his head.

Sweet Jesus. With the amount of testosterone his body emanated, all she wanted was to straddle his body and wallow in him until his hotshot attitude turned into white-hot passion. He challenged her, tugged at everything feminine inside her. And she wasn't quite sure how to handle it.

Sure, she worked in a male-dominated profession, and a lot of the men thought they were hot. But they weren't anything like this man laid out on her bed. They might be similar to Tate in their overconfident, swaggering persona. But Tate had more inside him than any man she'd ever met. His confidence was real, and his underlying compassion and kindness were human. And his rare moments of vulnerability were heart stopping. There were so many facets to him that Lara's head spun and her body hummed with need. She wanted to take him apart layer by layer, and figure out who the real Tate Colter really was...or if he was all of those things rolled together into one hot male.

She'd never been sexually aggressive, mostly because she'd never seen the sexual desire in a man's eyes the way she saw it in Tate's every time he looked at her. She knelt on the bed carefully and boldly cupped his groin. Her heart raced as she felt his hard erection beneath her fingers. She traced over it as she looked him directly in the eyes. "I wasn't using you. Last night was one of the most amazing experiences of my life. I didn't know it could be...like that."

All traces of humor left his face as his expression became intense. "You mean you never came that hard?" he asked in a voice harsh with passion.

"I mean I never came at all. Not with a man." She sighed as he gaped at her. "I've been with two guys in my life: my cheating ex-boyfriend and my first crush in my senior year of high school. The high school experience was painful and then it was...rushed. The cheating ex wasn't much into anybody's pleasure except his own." That made Tate special to her. He'd been so damn intent on making her come, focusing on her pleasure first. Sex like that could become highly addictive.

His strong hands wrapped around her waist and flipped her onto her back with one smooth motion. His body instantly covered hers. "Baby, a woman's pleasure should always come first." His expression became fierce and covetous.

"I'm different. I guess my ex saw me more as a federal agent," she whispered breathlessly.

"You're also a woman. All woman. I should know. I felt all of those soft, sexy parts last night. My only regret is I didn't get to taste you, bury my mouth in your pussy until you screamed for mercy," he answered huskily. His eyes searched her face. "Were you dressed to meet Marcus in the bar the other day? Were you trying to get his attention?"

"Yes," she admitted honestly. "My objective was to meet up with Marcus in any way possible and have him notice me. Then I wanted to get close to him and get any information I could get."

"How close?" Tate growled.

She sighed. "Not that close. I love my country and the citizens here, but my job stops after flirtation. I don't fuck men for information. This is an unusual assignment for me. Usually I'm not trying to attract a man's attention."

"You attracted me instead of Marcus," Tate rasped. "I still regret the things we didn't do, but I'll put my head between those soft thighs later."

Lara's eyes fluttered closed as she imagined that visual; her body vibrated with need. What would that be like? With Tate, it would probably be a surreal pleasure like she'd never known. "Be careful. I'm armed," she reminded him as her eyes flew open again.

"So am I. But the only danger you're in right now is from me," he growled. His mouth swooped down to take hers with a commanding swiftness that took her breath away.

Her arms went around his neck instinctively, and his masculine, musky scent captivated her, surrounded her until she couldn't think of anything except him. His taste, his dominance, his sensual demand that she yield to him all set her body on fire.

He finally released her mouth and yanked on the high neck of the black turtleneck sweater she wore. He moved it downward so he could leave a path of fire down her neck as his mouth consumed the sensitive flesh.

"Lara," he breathed against her temple. "You drive me crazy, baby."

She was just tilting her head to give him better access when a loud knock came from the door.

"Shit!" she exclaimed. Her heart pounded from Tate's sensual assault and the shock of being jolted back into the real world.

"Lara. Are you in there?" Chloe Colter's voice came through the locked door.

"Oh my God. It's your sister." Lara pushed gently at Tate's massive chest.

"Damn. She never did have good timing." Tate groaned as he reluctantly let her get up.

"I'm coming." Lara pulled her sweater down and tried to finger comb her tangled hair before she quickly confined it in a clip at the back of her head.

"I wish," Tate grumbled as he rolled to his feet.

A giggle actually escaped her lips before she stifled it. Tate's unhappy tone that they'd been interrupted actually delighted her.

He wants me. He really wants me.

It was one of the best natural highs she'd ever experienced. She wasn't used to a man who treated her like an attractive female instead of a federal agent, and it made her feel lighthearted and blissfully happy.

She walked to the door and flipped the lock. She opened it with a small smile, an expression that quickly fled as she looked at the man who stood next to Chloe.

Marcus Colter.

"Hi Chloe," she greeted Tate's smiling sister. "Mr. Colter?"

Another man stood on the other side of Chloe, and she didn't recognize him. He appeared to be about the same age as Marcus.

"Blake? I didn't know you were back." Tate's voice was more enthusiastic than it had been a few minutes ago.

The tenseness in Lara's muscles relaxed. *Not Marcus then.* She had been focused on photos of Marcus Colter for so long that she'd forgotten that he had an identical twin, Senator Blake Colter. Marcus was the oldest Colter brother, but only by minutes. Marcus and Blake Colter looked so much alike that Lara wondered how Tate could instantly tell them apart.

Obviously their siblings can easily tell which one is which. They grew up together.

"Senator," Lara said as she nodded at him. "It's nice to meet you, sir." She looked at Chloe. "And it's nice to see you again."

She stepped aside to let the three visitors through the door so Tate could greet his brother. He did so with a slap on the back and a typical Tate smart-ass comment. "It's nice of you to finally get your ass back here to actually see the people who voted for you."

Blake shoved back at his younger brother. "Introduce us," he told Tate with a grin as he looked back at Lara appreciatively.

"Don't even think about trying to charm her. She won't fall for your bullshit," Tate growled, sounding like he was only partially joking. "Lara, this is my brother, Blake, and his friend, Gabe Walker."

"Mr. Walker." She shook the man's hand.

"Gabe, please."

"And none of the formalities for me either, Lara. Please call me Blake. Any friend of my family is a friend of mine, too," he said charmingly.

I'm not so sure I'll be a friend to any of you once I bust your older brother.

In fact, she was pretty certain she was going to be the most hated person among the whole Colter family. Her heart clenched at what the conclusion of this investigation was going to do to them, especially Tate.

"I wanted to make sure you were okay," Chloe explained. "Tate texted me yesterday that he'd found you, but you weren't here earlier this morning."

"I—I was—"

"She was with me. My place was closer and she was stranded out in the cold," Tate told them smoothly.

"I'm glad you're okay," Chloe said with a smile.

Lara smiled back at the attractive brunette. Gabe Walker couldn't seem to take his eyes off Chloe. *Interesting.*

Blake looked at Tate, confused. "If you were at your place, why couldn't you just take the Jeep and p—"

Tate shoved his elbow into his brother's stomach.

"Ouch. What the hell was that?" Blake complained and rubbed his sore abdomen.

"Sorry," Tate apologized with a total lack of remorse. "Lara and I were just on our way out. We'll talk later." He gave his older brother a warning look to stop talking.

Lara watched the interaction between the two of them with interest, but let Tate take her hand and lead her to the door. She picked up her outdoor gear from the chair and handed Tate his jacket.

The three visitors left with promises to meet up at a later date, leaving Lara and Tate to follow.

"Did you say you were packing?" Lara asked, nervous about going out to the airfield and what they might find there. Tate had said Marcus had been delayed by weather and hadn't arrived yet, but wasn't sure when he was due to come in.

Tate turned his back to her. "Do you want to feel my gun?" His voice was full of innuendo.

After she pulled the door closed and dropped the plastic key into her pocket, she put a hand to his back. "Big gun," she commented as she felt the back holster before he put his jacket on.

"Baby, everything I have is big." He winked at her. "My hands are larger. I need at least a standard sized gun."

"Harder to conceal," she shot back at him as they walked down the hall to the elevator. "Bigger isn't always better."

"But in some cases it's definitely preferable." He wiggled his eyebrows at her as he waved her into the elevator first.

"Sometimes guys who have big things don't always have the best equipment. They're compensating."

"You know that definitely doesn't apply to me." He grinned at her, his eyes twinkling devilishly.

Wicked man. But she couldn't really argue much about *that*. Tate had absolutely nothing he needed to compensate for.

Their moods sobered as they exited the resort and Tate opened the passenger door of his heavy truck for her, another first. Guys didn't open doors for her…ever.

He jogged around to the driver's side and slid into the seat. "Let's get this over with. I can think of much more enjoyable things to do."

Lara swallowed hard to remove the lump from her throat. "Tate, I'm sorry—"

"Don't apologize," he rumbled. "Marcus has nothing to do with anything remotely illegal or harmful to anyone. I know my brother."

The evidence against Marcus Colter was irrefutable. The shipments had been purchased by him, and the cargo transported to Rocky Springs. It was killing her that Tate was going to be shattered, but it was unavoidable.

"I hope you're right," she answered simply, knowing he wasn't, but wishing that by some impossible miracle that he really *did* know his eldest brother better than the FBI.

Chapter 8

"I don't suppose you have a key," Lara asked Tate hopefully as she stood at the regular entrance door for the enormous new hangar that had been completed over the summer. She wrapped her arms around her body and hopped from one foot to the other to try to stay warm. The sun was out, and the day was crystal-clear after the storm, but it was bitterly cold.

"I don't need a key." Tate dug into the pocket of his jeans and pulled out a jackknife, extending a portion that had several different thin metal extensions.

"You're going to pick the lock?" Her teeth started to chatter.

He crouched down without answering and the door popped open in under a minute. "I wasn't breaking in. I was just opening a door on my property in an unconventional manner." Tate swung the door open and motioned her in. "You wanted in to take a look around... you're in." His voice was gruff as he put the knife back in his pocket.

Lara didn't argue as she stepped into the warm, enormous space. The hangar was large enough to house several planes or a couple of private jets. Right now the main space was empty except for maintenance equipment for the aircraft.

Her heart sank as she looked at Tate's remorseful expression. He might be convinced of his brother's innocence, but Lara could tell it didn't sit right for him to invade his brother's space without permission.

He crossed his arms in front of him. "Take your look around and let's get the hell out of here."

There was no aircraft parked in the gigantic space, so she was able to get around the large area quickly, bypassing a few small rooms with desks, obviously small offices.

Not a big enough area for a large amount of explosives.

She shucked her gloves and put them in the zippered chamber of her ski jacket so her hands would be free, and pulled her cell phone from the pocket of her jeans to send a text.

I'm in. Looking.

She'd called the director of her division as soon as she'd learned that she'd have access to a possible storage spot for the shipments of the explosives. Even though she was only conducting an investigation, looking for possible evidence, he'd wanted her to have backup available. There was no time to get her regular team here to Colorado from Washington DC, so her boss had connected her to a team that had been rapidly assembled and deployed from Denver. The airstrip was currently surrounded by federal officers in case she found anything during her search.

Every office was empty except for a desk, chair, or equipment storage for the planes and helicopters.

Until she reached a locked door.

"What's in here?" she called to Tate, who still stood near the exit door.

He strode over and tried the door himself. "I don't have a clue."

"Judging from the exterior, it's a pretty large space," Lara mused.

Tate crouched again and pulled out his knife to expertly pop the lock.

"Sheesh. Don't you guys have an alarm system here?" Lara asked curiously.

Tate shrugged as he pushed the door open. "What for? Like some-body is really going to come to the middle of the Rocky Mountains, who just happens to be a pilot, to steal a plane? And all of our em-ployees have been with us for years. We trust them."

Amazing. Where Lara came from, nobody trusted anybody. But she'd never lived in a small town before. And Rocky Springs was definitely remote. Their homes and the airstrip was a pretty good distance away from the actual resort.

She entered the room in front of Tate and stopped short; he bumped into her back. "Oh, God. What is all this?" Her eyes roamed around the enormous storage area.

Everything was crated, and there were too many crates to count. The gigantic storage room seemed crammed with stacked pack-ing boxes.

"One way to find out," Tate said grimly as he took out his knife to tear open one of the crates. "Fuck!" he rasped. The lid hit the cement floor with a loud clatter. "There's enough C4 here to cause some major damage."

Lara watched as Tate popped the lid on box after box, uncovering a huge collection of explosives, missiles, arms and equipment to assemble some major bombs. She blinked back tears as she pulled out her cell phone and sent a text.

Evidence found.

"It's not possible. This is not fucking possible," Tate raged as he continued to rip the tops off more crates.

"Tate, stop. Please." Lara couldn't stand to keep watching him, his torment almost tangible.

"Marcus didn't do this. He wouldn't do this." Tate dropped another lid on the floor and turned to her. "He wouldn't."

The fierce protectiveness in his expression nearly tore Lara apart.

"I'm afraid he did and he has done it," a masculine voice droned behind Lara.

She turned quickly, just in time to find herself staring down the barrel of several assault rifles, and at the face of Marcus Colter.

Marcus had the Colter trademark gray eyes, but they were currently emotionless, lifeless. He gave sharp orders in Arabic, mostly likely for both of them to be restrained. One thing she knew about Marcus Colter was that he was fluent in several languages, including Arabic. Her knowledge of the language was minimal, and she understood very little of what he said, but she could tell from his tone that he was issuing commands.

She and Tate were both restrained and disarmed in moments. Tate's knife dropped to the floor, along with her own two weapons and Tate's gun. They couldn't make a move: several assault rifles were ready to lay them flat and bloody in less than a heartbeat.

It was a strange situation: all six foreign men and Marcus dressed in suits, looking as though they'd just come from a business meeting. Maybe they had—a meeting about the business of terrorism. How many men in custom suits actually brandished assault rifles?

"Why?" Tate ground out as one of the men bound his hands behind him with twine. "Why in the fuck would you do this? Look at me, dammit. Look me in the face, Marcus, and tell me why you're doing this!"

Marcus didn't comply. He continued to look at Lara with lifeless eyes as he moved close to them, waiting for the other men to move away before he spoke English quietly to her and Tate. He kept his voice low, obviously wanting the conversation to be only between him and his brother. "Money. Everything is all about money, Tate. I've found out there's a fortune to be made in this business."

"Bullshit. You don't care about the money!" Tate exploded. "What about Dad?"

"He's dead," Marcus replied. "Life goes on."

"You don't give a shit about money. We all have so much we don't know what to do with it now."

"It's never enough. Money is also power," Marcus answered flatly as he nodded at Lara. "Who is this?"

Her hands now bound tightly behind her back, Lara glared at Marcus. "I'm your worst nightmare, Colter."

Marcus moved close enough to touch her. "Ah…another soul who is out to save the world? Law enforcement of some kind, I assume." He finally looked over at Tate.

"Don't even fucking touch her," Tate growled. "Let her go. She has nothing to do with this."

Lara knew Marcus wouldn't believe that for a minute after he'd seen how she was armed, and she wasn't about to leave Tate here after what had been found, even if Marcus would let her go.

"I want her before she dies." One of the men who held an assault rifle grunted in a heavy accent as the group came back to join Marcus again.

Just the thought of any one of these men touching her made her want to gag—and that included Marcus. She wanted to kill *him* just for the way he'd betrayed his family, much less his country.

One. Two. Three.

Lara counted the gun barrels that were aimed at her—three men with guns, four unarmed, including Marcus. And she and Tate had both been restrained. She liked to think she could handle anything as an agent, but her odds of surviving this situation were slim unless the Denver team of agents got inside the hangar pretty damn soon.

She watched as one of the unarmed men went and picked up Tate's blade, opened the knife portion and quickly split her turtleneck from the neck to the hem.

"Touch her and I'll fucking kill you," Tate bellowed furiously. He moved forward to head-butt the man who ripped her clothing.

The guy with the knife recovered quickly and went for Tate. Lara screamed, and kicked out with her leg as the man rushed Tate with his own blade. She deflected him, but the knife caught Tate in the shoulder. Both of them had been divested of their outerwear when they'd been stripped of their weapons. Tate had very little protection from the blade in his thin T-shirt, and the stab wound was immediately opened and bleeding.

Marcus moved forward and grabbed the man who had assaulted Tate by the collar of his suit jacket. "Are we here to make an inspection of the latest shipment or not?"

The terrorist shrugged off Marcus's grip and spoke sharply to the other two men who weren't holding a weapon. He must have wanted them to check out the explosives, because the men entered the storage room.

"I'll watch them, if you don't mind. Our discovery is going to require a change of plans now," Marcus commented blandly as he looked at the man who was obviously in charge of the other terrorists, the man who had gone for Tate.

Marcus didn't wait for an answer before he followed the two men into the storage room that contained the explosives. He obviously didn't care whether he got the leader's agreement or not.

Lara moved closer to Tate, trying to see how bad the wound on his shoulder was. It bled so profusely that she couldn't tell. He was losing blood, but his expression was one of fury rather than pain.

"Are you okay?" Tate whispered fiercely.

She nodded. "I'm worried about you."

"I've survived a hell of a lot worse. Can you untie me? I'm working on the knots, but it will go faster if you can help."

Lara was already trying to move slightly behind Tate while the men were occupied; the leader spoke rapidly to the men who held the assault weapons. She tried to turn discreetly to try to help Tate loosen his bound hands.

"Move away from him." The leader with the knife was back in front of them again in a heartbeat.

Dammit!

Lara moved obediently, not wanting Tate to be punished any further for trying to rescue her. She should have been more prepared for this scenario, should have watched for anyone to enter the hangar. But she'd made a tragic mistake: she'd gotten distracted emotionally. Her heart had broken as she watched Tate's sense of betrayal play out in front of her.

The leader had a punishing grip on her arm, and as she jerked to pull away, he grasped her by the hair and dislodged the clip that held the unruly locks away from her face. She winced in pain as he tugged hard to bring her in front of him, and then pushed on her skull. "Down. You will suck me now. If you do anything that doesn't feel good, your boyfriend is dead."

Boyfriend? Did he not know that Tate was Marcus's brother? She spoke very little Arabic, so she hadn't been able to make out the rapid-fire conversation Marcus had with the terrorists. Although this man obviously spoke some English, she didn't know about the others.

Nobody except me heard Marcus's conversation with Tate. It's weird that he didn't identify Tate as his brother.

Lara went down to her knees as the bastard tugged hard on her hair and forced her head down with the other hand. She gagged just from the thought of putting this murderous asshole's penis in her mouth. It was her nature to fight, but Tate's life was at stake, and he was already wounded. She'd do whatever she had to do to stall for time, even if she'd rather put her skull in his balls with every ounce of strength she had right now.

He fumbled with the fly on his pants with one hand, while he held her steady with her hair wrapped around his other beefy paw.

"Lara, goddammit, no!" Tate howled. He moved to lift his leg to take down Lara's tormenter.

He didn't make it. All three of the other men were needed to yank Tate back before he could take the terror boss off his feet with a swift kick. Tate had been ready to execute the move, but was jerked back just before he could swing his leg.

Lara never saw the hand coming toward her face because her eyes were on Tate; the man in front of her landed a powerful blow to her cheek. Her eyes teared from the stinging pain, and she tilted toward the side. Unable to keep her balance with her hands tied, she collapsed on the concrete floor sideways, only to be yanked back to her knees seconds later by her hair. "You move again and she gets punished for it," the leader grunted. He sent a warning, merciless glance at Tate.

Her head still whirled and her vision was blurry from the forceful blow her face had taken. Her skull had connected with the concrete when she'd fallen, which had further scrambled her brain. Lara stared at the erect penis in front of her face, almost glad her eyesight was fuzzy.

Don't think about it. Just do it. If I throw up on him while he's forcing me to suck him, he can't blame me for that. I just need time. Just a little more time and I know the team stationed around the airport will get in. I have to keep Tate alive.

"I swear to God that I'll cut your dick off and shove it down your throat if you don't let go of her," Tate growled.

"What the hell is going on out here?" Marcus's voice sounded across the room.

Keep everybody happy just a little longer.

Her captor jerked on her hair again to bring her face to his groin, and Lara struggled not to heave.

Then, suddenly she was free, released in a hail of gunfire that had her hitting the floor on purpose this time. She turned her head, terrified to look at Tate, but she had to know whether he was still alive.

Tate was free, and not only was he alive, but he'd obviously grabbed one of the men's guns and disarmed the other two. He held the weapon that had sent a hail of bullets straight into her attacker, the man lying dead on the floor not more than five feet away from her. He was panting and obviously furious, his eyes as hard as steel as he watched Marcus and the other two men fly out of the storage room. Both of the men at Marcus's side hesitated and picked up the guns that they had taken away from her and Tate.

Two of the guns they had were her weapons, so Lara knew they were both completely loaded.

"FBI! Drop your guns! Now!" The screaming male voice came from the entrance door.

Thank God. The team was finally here and inside the hangar.

The man who had grabbed her Glock 23 raised it toward the booming voice, and gunfire rang ferociously in the cavernous building.

Tate sprinted and flung himself on top of her, knocking the wind out of her body as he surrounded her head with his arms. Lara was stunned when she realized that *he* was protecting *her* with his body, making certain she wasn't hit by stray bullets.

The shooting stopped suddenly. The gunman with her Glock was dead on the floor. The other men raised their hands over their heads in surrender.

"Agent Bailey?" one of the agents called.

"Here," she answered loudly. "Don't shoot the guy on top of me. He's one of the good guys and he's injured. Please help him." Her voice was desperate. Tate was covered in blood, and it was all his own.

"I'm good," Tate told her in a low voice beside her ear. "You okay, baby?"

He *was* good, but he was far from healthy at the moment. Lara could hear the pain in his voice, but he wasn't going to show it. "I'm all right," she reassured him as he came to his feet and lifted her gently into a standing position and quickly untied her hands.

"You're bleeding and the bastard hit you so hard he left a hand-print on your face," he answered, enraged. He touched a finger lightly to her cheek and he swiped away a little blood.

Lara looked over at the dead man. "He's wearing a ring. I think it just caught my skin," she said dismissively as she reached out to rip his T-shirt and get a look at his wound.

Tate had blood soaking his T-shirt, on his face, and large stains on his jeans. There were also a few puddles on the floor. "You've lost too much blood. You need help." She put a hand firmly over the laceration that was right between his chest and collarbone, and put as much pressure as possible on the stab wound to stop the bleeding. She used her other hand to give her counter pressure on his back.

One of the team of agents ran over to them. "I think we have them all contained, Agent Bailey. There were seven total?"

"Yes. Including the dead guy on the floor. The use of deadly force was necessary," Lara told the tall, dark-haired agent who looked to be in his early thirties in a sharp, businesslike voice. "This is Tate Colter. He's Special Forces and he helped me out. He needs treatment. He was stabbed by one of the perps."

"You need us to carry you out to the car, Mr. Colter?" the agent asked, suddenly realizing the amount of blood Tate had lost. "We'll get you to the hospital." The agent glanced at Lara. "You look like you need to get checked, too. Your face is a mess."

Tate grunted. "Nobody carries me unless I'm dying or dead. Right now, I'm neither one of those things." He put an arm protectively around Lara. "Let's go."

She rolled her eyes. "I'm trying to hold pressure here," she told him angrily as his protective hold dislodged her hands from holding tension on his wound.

"It's fine. I want a doctor to look at your injuries. Let's get to the car," he growled as he steered her toward the entrance. The agent trailed right behind them.

Tate stopped suddenly near the door, his eyes murderous as he watched his brother approach, being led to the exit in handcuffs by a federal agent.

Lara's breath hitched and time seemed to stop as the two brothers finally looked at each other. She could feel Tate's whole body shudder as he slowly lowered his arm from around her shoulder and approached his brother.

Marcus looked as though he was barely affected by what was taking place, but his eyes were assessing as he watched Tate walk over to him.

Without a word, Tate drew his arm back and let his fist fly, punching his brother squarely in the face. The agent behind Marcus needed to steady him to keep Marcus on his feet.

"That's for betraying your country and letting Lara get hurt—you selfish prick," he said in a husky, menacing voice before he turned his back on Marcus and returned to Lara's side to grab her hand.

Tears rolled down her face. Her heart squeezed inside her chest at the betrayal that Tate was suffering from at the moment. It wouldn't end here. She knew that. Tate would be wounded more than physically from having his loyalty forsaken by his older brother.

She squeezed his hand in a show of support.

He pulled her forward and out of the hangar, never once looking back at Marcus as he got her into the car and the agent drove like a maniac toward the hospital.

Chapter 9

Gabe Walker swung his big pickup truck into a vacant spot along the main road of Rocky Springs, his gut in knots over what he had to do.

He exited the truck and shook his head slowly as he plopped his black Stetson on his head. People jokingly referred to him as the billionaire cowboy, but he never took offense. He'd lived most of his childhood in Texas, born wealthy because he had a father who had made his fortune in oil. Like Blake, his dad had also had a cattle ranch. So Gabe guessed he was as much a cowboy as any other, even more than Blake, who many referred to as the cowboy senator because he had a cattle ranch.

He paused at the door and looked at the neat, fancy script written on the pristine window of the business:

Chloe Colter, DVM

He still had a hell of a time believing that little Chloe Colter was now a doctor, and a damn good vet from what he'd heard.

And not so little anymore.

Gabe could easily admit to himself that the woman got his dick hard. She had ever since she'd come back to town and he'd seen her again over a year ago, all grown up and filled out in all the right places. She was a beautiful woman, and she got riled up every time he was around. Okay…yeah…maybe she had reason to dislike him a little. But it wasn't looking as if she was going to get over the incident they'd had any time soon.

He released a masculine sigh as he pulled the door open and approached the reception desk of Chloe's clinic, his mind back on his task.

Hell, how could he tell her about what was happening when he didn't really understand everything himself?

"What are *you* doing here?" The receptionist seat was empty and Chloe popped her pretty head around the corner. She glared at him as she spoke.

He took his hat off and motioned her out into the waiting room, which was empty. It was after business hours, but as usual, Chloe was still working with her animals. "I have to talk to you, Chloe."

She must have reacted to the grave tone of his voice, because she flew out the door of the reception area immediately. "What?" She closed the door behind her and stood in front of Gabe with a questioning look on her face.

Oh hell, she looked so beautiful. He swallowed the lump in his throat as he looked down at her.

Just tell her. It isn't going to get any easier.

"Tate's injured. He's at the hospital," he told her in a husky voice.

Her face fell. A distressed look took the place of her curious expression. "Oh my God. How bad? What happened? Is he going to be all right?"

He didn't know much. Blake had gotten a call, and Gabe had been at his house discussing some ranching issues when he'd gotten the news that Tate had been injured, and that most of the airstrip on Colter property was being sectioned off as a crime scene while the FBI investigated.

"I don't know. I'll take you to the hospital. Blake went to pick up your mom."

He told her about the injury that had occurred at the airstrip, and that access was restricted into some of that area for now as a crime scene.

"Why?" Chloe gaped at him. "Did he crash?"

Gabe shook his head. "All I know is that he was apparently stabbed by an unknown person. It's an FBI investigation, and we don't know a whole lot more." He took a deep breath before adding, "One more thing, Chloe."

Jesus H. Christ. How could he tell her about the other tragedy for her family when she was already afraid for Tate? But he had to do it. "Your brother Marcus has been arrested."

Chloe put her hands on her hips. "Please tell me this is all some kind of sick joke. That's not possible. Marcus is as moral as a man can be. What in the world could he get arrested for?"

Gabe had thought the same thing, but it was apparently true. "The FBI has him in custody for conspiring to commit an act of terror." Christ, he could hardly believe it himself. He didn't know Marcus as well as he knew Blake, but never in his wildest dreams could he see a straight arrow like Marcus flying crooked.

"Please tell me you're joking," Chloe pleaded. Her eyes grew bright with tears.

"I might be an asshole sometimes, Chloe, but I swear I wouldn't joke about something like this. I'm sorry." He couldn't stand to see those vulnerable gray eyes look at him pleadingly. He wanted to tell her that he wasn't serious, but he couldn't. He was as serious as a heart attack. "Grab your coat, darlin', and I'll drive you to the hospital to check on Tate."

"Yeah. Yeah, I'll get it." Chloe look dazed as she opened the door and reached back into the office for her winter gear and her purse.

Gabe took it from her and helped her into the jacket, taking her hat and pulling it gently over her ears and wrapping her scarf around her neck.

"Can you drive fast, please?" she begged him as they stepped outside and she tried to lock her office door with a shaky hand.

He took the key from her, locked the deadbolt, and dropped the key ring into her purse. "As fast as I safely can," he promised as he opened the door of his truck and helped her inside.

She still looked as if she was in shock, so he buckled her up before he gently closed the door and ran around to the driver's seat.

Once settled, he started the truck up and started the short drive to the hospital. He took the icy roads as fast as he dared, which was pretty damn far over the speed limit.

"I don't know what to think. I don't know how to believe this," Chloe murmured quietly.

"Everything will be okay, Chloe. We'll get it all figured out as soon as we get to the hospital. Tate will be all right. You know he's too dang ornery to be down for long." Gabe hoped to hell he was right.

"I'm worried about Mom. She isn't going to take this very well. Even if Tate is okay, Marcus being charged with something that ludicrous is going to hurt her."

"We don't know what happened. Let's find out the facts first. Maybe it's all a misunderstanding. Blake said the agent who called wasn't very forthcoming."

She let out a deep, breathy sigh, as if she was trying to calm herself down. Gabe could see her hand tremble as she rested her arm on the console between them. He didn't stop to think. Reaching out, he clasped her shaky hand in his and squeezed it lightly. "Breathe, Chloe."

She took another deep breath. Gabe was surprised when she didn't pull away. She entwined their fingers together and clung to his hand, trusting him as she nodded.

His heart banged against his chest wall, and he stroked her hand with his thumb. It was as if Chloe had given him the world when she'd clasped his hand. And maybe she had...because she was comforted by his touch, and she was giving him her trust.

Just this...only this brief moment in time meant everything to him.

Holding her hand is better than the best sex I've ever had in my life.

As Gabe pulled into the parking lot of the hospital, he hoped to hell things weren't as bad as they seemed right now. But if they were...he would somehow, someway, make everything right for Chloe again.

He hated to break their fragile connection as he parked the truck, but they both hopped out, eager to get inside.

He held his hand out as she stepped over a parking block; Chloe reached out and clasped it again. Gabe entwined their fingers as they jogged toward the entrance, glad that he was here to support Chloe, but wondered why she hadn't bothered to call her fiancé.

"I want to get the hell out of here…now," Tate grumbled as he tried to sit up on the gurney in the emergency room of the Rocky Springs Medical Center.

Blake, Chloe, Tate's mother, and Gabe Walker all hovered at the end of the single bed in the room.

Lara was right beside Tate, and she pushed him gently but firmly back down to the pillow. "You're not leaving right now. You need to finish the IV they're giving you. You lost too much fluid."

Thankfully, nothing important had been damaged, and Tate had needed nothing except fluid replacement, meds, and a whole lot of sutures to close his wound.

"I'm outta here," Tate informed her testily. "Hell, I've lost more blood when I donate a pint."

Lara could debate what Tate was saying, but she didn't bother. She leaned in close to him and put her mouth against his ear to whisper sensually, "If you behave, I promise I'll give you a blowjob later that will make your head want to explode."

Okay…she wasn't exactly an expert at oral sex, but Tate didn't need to know that. She pulled back from him, her face right in front of his and deliberately licked her lips.

Tate caved immediately and lay back down against the pillow. "I'm staying until the IV is done," he agreed hastily.

Lara smiled at him. "Thank you."

"Sit down," he demanded. "You look like you need to be in this bed worse than I do. The son of a bitch did a number on your face."

Lara had seen her reflection, and it wasn't pretty. Nothing was broken, but her jaw and cheek were swelled and had started to bruise. They'd cleaned up the small cut on her cheek and it was barely noticeable. "I've survived a hell of a lot worse." She mimicked his earlier words, but she pulled up the chair beside the bed and sat down near his head.

"Do I even want to know what you just said to make him stay?" Blake drawled warily from the end of the bed.

Lara turned her head to look at Tate's family. Blake and Chloe still looked as though they were in shock over the entire situation, Gabe's expression was grim, and Tate's mother cried silently. Tears poured down Aileen's face, but she kept her mouth firmly closed.

"I told him that you and Gabe would physically restrain him." Lara lied her ass off.

Tate snorted. "If that was what you'd really said, I'd be hightailing it out of here by now. Those two wouldn't stop me."

Lara gave Tate a warning look, and changed the subject. "Some of the agents brought Tate's truck here to the hospital. I can take him home when he's finished here. I know this has been a stressful day. Maybe you should all go get some rest."

"I'd like to see Marcus." Aileen finally spoke in a tremulous voice.

"He's already being transported back to the FBI headquarters in DC. He's a bit of a special case, and the Denver agents said they got orders from higher up the ladder to get him to Washington as soon as possible. I'm sorry, Mrs. Colter. He'll get a trial, and you'll be able to see him eventually." The pain in the older woman's eyes made Lara want to weep. Marcus's crimes had literally destroyed this whole family. They were all broken apart. The Colters were a respected family, an admired family, and they would all end up being hurt by what Marcus had done.

"I have to get to Washington, too," Blake said in a quiet, grave tone. "They want me for questioning. I wouldn't be surprised if we all end up needing to testify eventually."

"Are you under suspicion?" Tate asked angrily. "Guilty by association. Shit. This will kill your career once it gets out, Blake, even if you're not guilty of a damn thing."

Blake shook his head slowly. "The last thing I care about is my political career right now," he answered, his eyes full of sadness and concern. "I know you saw it with your own eyes, Tate, but I guess I still want to be in denial that Marcus is guilty."

"Me too," Aileen whispered in a tearful voice.

"And me," Chloe added.

Blake put an arm around his sister and mother, his expression bleak.

"I wish I could say the same," Tate uttered regretfully. "But I did see the whole thing, and he isn't the brother I've always known. I don't know what happened to him."

Lara reached out and clasped Tate's hand, feeling his emotional pain. Dear God, no matter how quickly he'd capitulated to her in exchange for sensual pleasure, Tate had to resent her somewhere deep inside him for tearing his family apart.

Chloe and Aileen moved to the other side of the bed and gave Tate a gentle embrace as Blake announced that he wanted to get his mom back home. Gabe offered to drive Chloe.

"Somebody needs to watch over Tate," Chloe said adamantly. "He might act like a hotshot, but he's going to need some help. I'll stay with him."

"Lara will stay." Tate kissed his sister on the forehead before she straightened. "Could you have some of the staff gather her belongings from the resort and send them to my place?"

"Gabe and I will handle it," Chloe agreed as she looked at Gabe for confirmation.

Gabe nodded quickly in agreement.

"Thanks." Tate looked at his family as he spoke. "This isn't going to break us. We're Colters, and we'll ride this out together."

Lara watched as Aileen's backbone straightened. "Yes, we will."

"Damn right we will," Blake acknowledged.

"We'll get through this," Chloe affirmed.

"Your friends will help." Gabe slapped Blake on the back.

Lara marveled at the strength she could feel in the small room. There was sadness, but a resilient spirit was also present. They all grieved right now, but she had no doubt they'd fight their way through this storm.

She watched them until they all left the room and closed the door behind them.

"You'll really stay with me?" Tate asked with atypical vulnerability in his husky voice.

Lara had already spoken with her boss, told him she needed time to heal and to help the Colter family. He'd told her to take some time off. "As long as you need me," she replied. Her eyes met his; she wished she could absorb some of the hurt that was still reflected in his gaze.

"Were you serious about that blowjob?" he asked hopefully.

"When you're healed." She tried to suppress a small smile.

"No...when *you're* healed," Tate answered hotly. His eyes roamed over her swollen face.

She moved closer to him, and rested her head gently on his abdomen, on top of the pristine white sheet. She felt emotionally wiped out, and so damn grateful that Tate was still alive. "I was scared," she admitted in a guilty whisper.

Maybe she wasn't supposed to feel that afraid as a federal officer, but she'd been terrified that Tate would end up dead. She took that risk herself every day doing her job, and she'd meet her fate if that's what it took to get terrorists off the street. But her fear and guilt she'd felt about getting Tate involved was the part she couldn't get over. To her, he was technically a civilian, and she'd gotten him involved in an FBI investigation that had nearly gotten him killed.

"In that particular situation, you'd have to be insane or completely stupid *not* to be afraid. You're neither of those things, baby. It's a natural reaction." He slid his hand through her disheveled hair and massaged her scalp. "You're the bravest, gutsiest woman I've ever known."

Lara sighed and let her body relax for the first time since that morning, and savored the unexplainable connection she had with Tate until the nurse came in to check his IV and got Tate ready to go home.

Chapter 10

"**W**ere you really going to let that bastard put his dick in your mouth?"

Lara looked up at Tate from her position beside him on his big bed. Her head rested on his abdomen. They'd had a quiet day today after the last several days of the madness of talking to the FBI and trying to unravel everything that had happened in this terrorist attempt. They'd arrived at Tate's home from the hospital four nights ago, both of them nearly falling asleep on impact when they hit the bed. Lara hadn't questioned following Tate into his bed. She'd wanted to sleep with him, know he was there beside her and breathing. It had become their habit every night; neither one of them even considered sleeping apart. Tate's wound was still healing, but sleeping together, having him hold her possessively in his arms every night, almost seemed more intimate than having sex.

The first day after the incident had been chaotic. After that, they'd done nothing more strenuous than play with Shep and visit with Chloe and her mom, who had come over every day to check in on Tate.

Blake was already gone, on his way to Washington.

"Yes, I would have done it," she finally answered. Tate's eyes turned territorial as he squeezed her waist. They'd spoken about the facts of the incident, but very little about the emotional toll it had taken on him.

Tate's bedroom was illuminated by the fire in the big stone fireplace across the room from the bed, but Lara knew some of the sparks coming from his gaze were fury and not a reflection of the firelight.

"Why?" he answered huskily. "You knew the team was coming. You could have nailed the bastard even though your hands were tied. It's doubtful that either of the other assholes would have shot you."

"Because they would have killed *you*," she admitted. His eyes softened as she spoke. "I would have let him rape me before I would have let them shoot you. I needed to buy some time. I did know the team was coming because I had texted them before they caught us." Tate already knew that because they'd hashed over all the details of what had happened the day Marcus had been arrested, but he was finally delving into the personal, and talking about that was much harder than the actual criminal facts.

He grasped her chin gently and turned her face sideways so he could look at the mark the criminal had left on her face. It was now faded, nearly gone. "Don't you know it would have killed me to watch that, see a man violate you that way?"

"You didn't have to watch it." She took his hand from her chin and entwined it with hers to rest their conjoined fingers beside her head. She wasn't going to argue with him, but she'd do it the same way all over again. "I would have healed, and I'm on birth control even though I'm not in a relationship because being violated or raped as a female agent is always a small risk. You wouldn't have healed. You would have been dead. It was my fault you were even there, that I got you involved. It never should have happened. You were Marcus's brother."

"Hey. Stop," he insisted. "Do you think I'm pissed off at you?"

"You should be. It would be normal to resent the woman who broke up your family." She put her head back on his stomach, not wanting to read his expression.

His hand sifted gently through her hair. "You did not break up my family. Jesus, Lara. Do you really think I could blame you for doing your job? Do you think I would have traded people's lives just to protect my brother?"

She couldn't stop herself. She tilted her head and looked into his eyes to see the truth. "No," she answered honestly as she saw the ferocity of his expression.

"No matter how much I care about my brother, the right thing had to happen. You didn't hurt my family. Marcus did. I'm glad he was busted before any lives were lost. My mom is hurting, but it would have killed her if her son had ended up being a mass murderer."

He doesn't hate me. He doesn't resent me. He doesn't blame me at all. God, he's an amazing man.

"Thank you for not blaming me."

"It. Was. Not. Your. Fault," Tate ground out. "Christ, you were willing to let some dirt bag violate you to keep me from dying."

"How did you disarm both of those guys and manage to get the gun away from the other one?" She wished she could have seen Tate's lightning-fast actions that had disarmed three men at once and killed a fourth one with their own gun. And he'd already been wounded.

"Desperation and training," he growled. "There was no way you were putting that beautiful mouth on that asshole. I'd have to be dead first."

The vehemence and savageness in his declaration made her heart skip a beat. When had anyone ever cared about her that much? Certainly, the agents in her team were like friends, and they'd protect her as much as she'd be willing to protect them. But none of them had this wild possessiveness toward her, this raw desire to keep her safe. "I didn't want you to be dead."

"What did you want me to be?" he rasped.

"Exactly like you are right now." Dressed in only a pair of flannel pajama bottoms, his usual *fuck-me* hair that seemed to occur every day from pulling on a winter hat to take Shep outside, Tate was every woman's wet dream. His body was hard beneath hers, and when his smoky eyes flared with heat, he was irresistibly, impossibly, undeniably the sexiest man alive. Tate Colter would always be just a little too cocky, arrogant, and untamed. But she liked him that way because he was also kind, sweet, and gentle: traits that were hidden beneath a hardened exterior. Sometimes he was a conundrum, but Lara understood him more and more every day.

Because we're so damn much alike.

Nothing and nobody had tugged at her feminine instincts like Tate did. She'd spent years being tough, trying to keep pace in a male-dominated profession. She couldn't afford to be anything except businesslike and impersonal, better than everyone else at what she did because she *was* a woman, and she had lived for her job for a very long time.

I want to live for myself, just for a little while.

She pulled herself up on her elbows and stared down at Tate's perfect, muscular body. The flannel nightgown she wore was far from sexy, but he still looked at her as if she were a *Playboy* centerfold and he was a horny teenager.

"I think I made you a promise when you were in the hospital that I'd like to fulfill right now," she said seductively. Her finger ran down his muscular chest. She had wanted to lay her hands on this man, pleasure the hell out of him, since the moment she'd made that vow.

"Not until your face is healed," he demanded roughly.

"It doesn't hurt." Lara loved seeing the hunger in his eyes.

"Then kiss me," he challenged as he speared a hand through her hair.

Careful not to lean on his chest, she leaned down and let him pull her mouth to his. She might have been the instigator, but Tate immediately took control. He licked, bit, and teased her lips before his tongue slid into her mouth to conquer her completely. She moaned against his lips, her tongue eagerly bantered with his.

He ravaged.

She surrendered without a fight, opened to him as he claimed her mouth as his, tenderly but dominantly. Her body caught fire as she became tangled in a web of desire so potent that her entire body trembled with need.

B. A. Scott

This is exactly how a kiss should be.

It should always be as life-altering as the assault to her senses was from Tate's embrace right now.

Her hand crept down his abdomen, relishing every defined muscle and indentation her fingers stroked over as she explored him. Finally, she jerked the drawstring on his pajama bottoms, eager to touch him.

Tate ripped his mouth from hers. "Lara, don't. I want you too damn bad right now, and your face is still healing."

"I don't need my face," she purred. "Just my mouth. And my cheek feels fine. The swelling is gone and it's painless."

She made contact with his enormous, erect member immediately because Tate was commando, nothing but flannel covering his hard erection. As she moved down to his knees, she yanked on his pajama pants. "I want you naked," she said boldly. She didn't want anything between her and Tate right now, and she quickly pulled the flannel nightgown over her head to reveal her bare body underneath. Her confidence faltered as she heard a low, reverberating sound come from Tate's mouth. But as she glanced at his expression, it was pure molten heat; his covetous eyes devoured her body.

She tugged on his pants, even more eager to feel the proof of his arousal. His cock popped out of the material as she drew it down; Tate lifted his ass to help her.

"My leg is scarred up," he said in a warning voice.

Tate actually had small scars everywhere, according to his history in the Special Forces, but they made him look like a warrior, and they made him even more dangerous and attractive. Although Lara winced for the pain every one of them had probably caused him, they didn't make him one tiny iota less desirable. They were part of Tate. And Tate was beyond perfection to her.

His leg was scarred, and she gasped as she pulled the pants from his feet and tossed the flannel to the floor. "Oh, God, this must have hurt like hell." She traced the healed dark scars lovingly.

Tate moved to put his leg under the covers at the bottom of the bed, but she grabbed it before he could hide it, and kissed the scars as she made her way up his lower body. "Don't. There isn't one thing about you that I don't find incredibly hot," she told him in a husky, shaky voice. He'd gained these scars saving lives, protecting their country, and no doubt by doing a mission that was incredibly risky. "You're my hero, Tate Colter." She palmed his cock as she moved next to his hips.

"Christ, Lara. You're killing me," he grumbled in a tormented voice.

She smirked at him as she lowered her head. "Then I guess I'll just have to bring you back to life."

Lara wasn't exactly incredibly experienced with tasting a man, even though she'd bragged to Tate to make him stay in the hospital. Instinct took over as she twirled her tongue around the tip of him and licked the droplet of moisture from the head. She closed her eyes, and savored the taste of him: warm, masculine, and heady. After she licked up the inside of the shaft, she finally took him into her mouth; his member was so large that there was no way she could take him completely. She wrapped her fingers around the base of the shaft, and moved them in time with her mouth as she devoured him.

Tate's tortured groan made her pussy clench almost painfully, and she became completely consumed, tightened her suction around his cock, and moved faster and faster.

"Dammit, Lara. I'm going to explode." Tate speared his fingers through her hair and guided her faster, harder.

He let go of her head to give her a chance to escape, but Lara wasn't going anywhere. She took him as deeply as possible. Tate's release pulsated into her throat, and she continued to stroke as he had an orgasm that had him crying her name in a hoarse, raw voice. "Lara."

His breathing was hard and heavy as he speared his hand back into her hair, massaging her scalp as he caught his breath. "Damn, you were right. My head did blow off," he rasped. He pulled her up beside him and flipped her on her back.

Stunned, Lara looked up at him in surprise. He changed their positions so fast that she hadn't even seen it coming. "What are you doing?" He had her hands pinned over her head.

His eyes shone like liquid silver. His big body now covered hers.

"I have to watch you come now, baby. I need to hear you moaning your pleasure while I taste your sweet pussy." His hand moved between their bodies; his fingers probed her folds.

She was saturated and slick, and Tate let out a satisfied grunt. "You're already wet. Getting me off turned you on?"

"Yes," she told him breathlessly. Her entire body quivered beneath his with a need so powerful that she could hardly catch her breath.

"Good. Because I'm going to enjoy the hell out of this, too." He lowered his head and kissed her. His dominant nature surfaced as he held her wrists fast and ravaged her mouth like he owned it.

"Don't hurt yourself," Lara pleaded when Tate let go of her lips to run his tongue along the sensitive skin of her neck.

"Baby, this isn't going to hurt for either one of us," he answered in a husky voice against her skin. "All I want is to taste you until you forget about anything except me."

Heat flooded between her thighs at the sound of Tate's demanding, sexy voice. He was in his element when he was sexually dominant, true to his nature, and his raw passion ramped up her desire to the boiling point. Here, she could let him take control of her body, trust him to pleasure her until she nearly lost her mind. She didn't have to be in control right now, and all she did was relax into his caresses and feel.

He released her wrists; his mouth moved to her breasts, and he teased one of her pebbled nipples with his teeth and tongue. "These are fucking perfect," he growled against her breast. His large hand cupped one and then the other, stimulating her hypersensitive peaks until she couldn't stand it anymore.

"I need you," Lara moaned. Her hands gripped the sheets as her back arched in pleasure. "Fuck me, Tate."

"Believe me, baby, I plan on it. Eventually," he answered gutturally. His mouth moved in sensual licks, nips, and erotic kisses to her abdomen. "Right now I just want to brand you as mine."

His tone was ravenous and greedy, as though he couldn't get enough of touching her. Those words from any other man might have been almost scary. But not from Tate. Never from Tate. He was protective and thoughtful, possessive and vulnerable, rough and heartbreakingly tender. Bossiness was second nature to him, and she understood that. She'd gladly hand him control so she didn't have to think for a while. She trusted him, she understood him, and that made all the difference in the way she reacted to his words.

She breathed a sigh of relief as he finally parted her thighs, his heated breath so close to her sex that it made her shiver in anticipation.

"You're killing me." She moaned his earlier words intentionally.

He took her hands and placed them on her breasts. "Pleasure yourself, baby."

All thoughts of modesty were gone, replaced by her body's cry for stimulation. She cupped her breasts, pinched her nipples ruthlessly to try to make the aching need throbbing inside her subside.

"You look beautiful like this," Tate growled. "So needy for me. So ready for me to satisfy you."

"Yes. Do it, dammit. I need you." Her body was coiled tightly, her desperation for Tate out of control.

"Time to revive you," he told her fiercely, but with a touch of humor that he sent similar words that she had said to him right back at her.

Lara's ass lifted at the first touch of Tate's mouth. He delved through her folds and into her pussy just like he did everything: totally focused, wild, and completely relentless. His sensual assault was erotic and carnal: his lips, teeth, tongue and nose completely buried in her pussy as he pushed her legs apart even farther to give him deeper access. His tongue rolled from bottom to top on her tender, pink flesh over and over again. He brushed the tiny bundle of nerves with every pass of his tongue, and her body ached to climax.

"Oh. God." She had never felt anything as raw and hot as Tate's mouth between her thighs; his lustful groan of enjoyment vibrated against her clit. She abandoned her breasts and fisted his short hair. "Yes, yes, yes," she chanted. Her entire body reacted to what he was doing to her; her channel clenched painfully.

He flicked his tongue over her sensitive, engorged bud and focused on her clit as he pushed two fingers into her channel, finally filling her. She clamped down on his fingers as he curled them around her g-spot, massaged it, and then retreated to enter her again and again.

Her back arched and her head thrashed on the pillow as Tate continued to tease her clit in the same rhythm as he moved his fingers in and out of her slick sheath. "Tate, I can't take it. I can't." The pleasure was so volatile that she felt as if she was ready to shatter.

She squeaked as he moved his other hand beneath her ass, teasing a finger between the cheeks of her ass. She was so wet that her juices easily coated the finger that he used to tease her anus, and eased the tip of it into the tight opening.

He was testing her limits, and Lara comprehended that—in the tiny corner of her mind that could still function. He teased and probed, never ceasing the motion of his tongue and the fingers that fucked her mercilessly. Every sensation Tate created was new and intense, and she had no boundaries with him. Everything he did to her had her ready to explode.

The tension in her body snapped. The coil in her belly unwound as her body pulsated violently. "Tate!" she screamed up toward the ceiling. His name turned into a long moan of pleasure as she had a climax like she'd never experienced before. She held onto his hair as her channel clenched tightly around his fingers. Spasms rocked her body as she arched her neck and rode the waves of her orgasm.

She panted through the remaining ripples of pleasure as Tate lapped at her climax and grunted in satisfaction against her pussy. His hands slid up her body. Both of them now coated with perspiration, they seemed to melt and sizzle into each other from the heat of their flesh.

Claiming her mouth the second he came up over her again, Tate kissed her roughly, and then tenderly. Lara tasted herself on his lips. She wound her arms around his back, relishing the feel of his hard, hot, demanding body on top of hers.

His cock entered her before his lips even left hers, and he buried himself to the root inside her.

She whimpered as he filled her, the sensation so sublime that she dug her short nails into his back.

"Fuck, yeah. Mine. You're mine, baby. This is all for me," he said harshly, possessively, staying buried as deeply as he could get inside her.

She wrapped her legs tightly around his waist and held him inside her. "It's all for you," she panted, knowing it was true. No man had ever made her feel the way Tate did, and most likely never would. Every action, every motion was elemental and feral. Her body strained to make this man join with her, belong with her. She claimed him as surely as he possessed her. "Fuck me. Please." Her body trembled, ached for Tate.

He pulled back until he was almost out and powerfully entered her again. "I need you so damn much." His declaration was animalistic and vulnerable at the same time.

She stroked her hands up and down his back as she felt his big body shudder. His cock entered and retreated in a fast, hard motion that satisfied her desperation for him. "Yes. Harder." Lara wanted the punishing force, the pummeling rhythm. This was like an affirmation that they were both alive after what had happened at the airstrip, and her body quivered as Tate shifted positions; his cock pressed against the sensitive area inside her that set off another climax.

She clenched his back again. Her nails bit into his skin to keep her grounded as her hips rose to receive every thrust of his cock. Her walls clenched him as she came; her muscles around his cock tightened on him, milking him.

"That's right, sweetheart. Let go. Come for me," he demanded harshly as he continued to pound into her. He groaned as he entered her one more time and found his own release.

They came down together in a mass of tangled sweaty arms and legs. Tate rolled off her, but kept one of his legs between hers. His arms wrapped around her waist and shoulders; he entwined his fingers in her hair and held her head against his chest protectively.

Lara rested against him. Her breath still came hard between her lips, her body completely sated, knowing that Tate had just changed her life irrevocably. "I didn't know it could be that intense," she admitted breathlessly.

"Me neither," Tate said huskily.

He drew her head back gently, tugging lightly on her hair as he laid a gentle kiss on her lips that made her heart skitter with an unfamiliar emotion that she didn't recognize at first. Then she realized that it was an emotion she hadn't felt in a long time—it was happiness.

Chapter 11

T ate knew he was screwed, and not in the good way.

The next morning, he watched as Shep sniffed along the edge of the woods and looked for the perfect place to do his morning thing. He held the leash lightly, letting the pup explore.

She's going to leave eventually. She doesn't belong here.

Problem was, Tate wanted Lara here, and if she left, it would completely gut him. His damn chest already ached every time he thought about Marcus, still not quite able to accept what his eldest brother had done. The thought of Lara leaving to return to Washington would eviscerate him.

He'd never really thought he was lonely until he'd met her. He'd always preferred to be alone. But now he could admit it...something vital had been missing from his life, and that *something* was actually *someone*—Lara.

The thought of her kneeling before that terrorist bastard, ready to do anything to save his life, messed with his head and humbled him completely. Fuck knows what he would have done if he'd had to watch her be violated. It had nearly killed him just to see another man touch her, and it was some dickhead terrorist.

She's a strong woman.

Yeah, his woman *was* a kick-ass female, but she also yielded to him so sweetly in bed that his cock got hard just thinking about the night before. She was a seductress, but in some ways so damn innocent. The combination of those two things tied him up in knots with wanting her. Just her reaction as he'd fingered her ass told him she was innocent in many ways. He'd never been much of an ass man, but Lara made him want every single part of her, greedily and completely. In fact, he craved her like a damn addiction, barely able to disentangle his body from hers to get out of bed when Shep had been whining to go outside.

I never knew it could be that intense.

Tate could still hear her saying those breathy, sexy words to him, and remembered how much they had affected him. Hell, he hadn't known it could be quite like that either, and he was probably a lot more experienced than she was. He'd had his share of women, but never had it been anywhere close to what he experienced with Lara.

Maybe I can fuck her out of my system.

As soon as he thought about that idea, he dismissed it. Lara was like crack to him. The more he got, the more he wanted.

He let out a masculine sigh as Shep finally found his pissing spot. It was so cold he could see his breath in the crisp air, but it would be a decent flying day because the weather was sunny and clear. He'd promised Lara he'd fly her into Denver later to file some reports at the FBI office. Hell, he'd be willing to do just about anything if it would keep her here longer. She'd pointed out that she could easily drive, but Tate was of the mind that flying was always preferable. It saved time, especially in the winter on mountain highways, and he'd rather be in the air than on the road any day.

Shep finished his business and hopped back through the snow and toward the house.

Smart dog. It's damn cold out here.

By the time he took off his boots and came back into the house, Lara was up, and she didn't look happy. He let Shep off the leash and hung it up. The puppy bounded over to Lara instantly. She picked him up and shuddered as she cuddled him against her breasts.

Lucky dog.

"You're cold," she crooned to the puppy, stroking his fur.

She was in his robe again, and a possessive satisfaction stabbed him straight in the gut. He liked his things draped over her body. Yeah, he preferred it to be his body over hers, but he'd take what he could get.

"What's wrong?" he asked her roughly, worried by her pensive expression.

She raised a brow at him. "You have a Jeep and a snowplow?"

Oh, hell. Busted!

"Yeah. Out in the other garage."

"So tell me exactly why I was snowed in here when you could have taken me back to the resort pretty easily."

Tate wasn't going to bullshit her. She looked pretty miffed. "Because I wanted you here. We were in the middle of a blizzard, Lara. Even if I did have a plow, it wasn't exactly safe to be out that night." He wasn't going to tell her that he'd gone out and plowed himself out in worse weather. The truth was...he'd wanted her to stay. And he hadn't wanted to take her out in the cold just to get her back to the resort. "You were hurt."

She crossed her arms in front of her. "You could have told me," she said, sounding disappointed.

Damn. Disappointed was worse than her being pissed off. "I could have," he said carefully.

"I don't like lies, Tate, for whatever reason."

He didn't like them either, especially between him and Lara, so he could understand her point. "I didn't lie exactly. I just didn't tell you I had a plow."

"A lie by omission, Colter," she told him sternly. "You didn't tell me because you didn't think about it. You didn't tell me because you didn't want me to know."

She was right. "I'm sorry. I appreciate honesty, too. I would have told you eventually."

"Don't do it again," she told him in a voice that reminded Tate of his fifth-grade teacher, and that woman had been pretty scary.

Lara put the puppy down and strode into the kitchen without another word.

Tate followed curiously. He watched as she went through the motions of fixing breakfast.

"I won't lie to you ever again, Lara." He meant that statement with his entire being. Now that he knew her better, he'd never be able to avoid laying everything on the table with her.

"Good." She nodded at him and went back to fixing breakfast.

"That's it?" She wasn't going to fry him over the issue?

"That's it. Now that I've made myself clear, I trust you to honor what I want." She caught his gaze for a short moment. "Besides, you did probably save my life, or at the very least having to touch that disgusting man. And you're almost disgustingly perfect. I guess you're due one mistake."

"Almost perfect?" Damn, he loved it when she teased him. "What would make me absolutely perfect?"

She pretended to study him for a minute. "You could learn to cook," she replied in a smart-ass tone.

He moved over to her and slapped her on the ass just to hear her cute little squeal. "Baby, nobody deserves to eat my cooking." But damned if he didn't want to try harder to learn because of her. She didn't deserve to do *all* of the cooking. "But I know every good restaurant in Colorado, and I can get us there fast. You don't have to cook."

"Hmm…I suppose there is that," she answered cheekily.

"I'll take you anywhere you want to go." He kissed her lightly on the temple and breathed in her intoxicating scent.

"After breakfast, I need to go to the resort. I just told Chloe I'd meet her in the gym. I hope it's not crowded by then."

Tate groaned. "Chloe ratted me out, didn't she?" His sister had been the one to tell Lara he had a snowplow.

"Not on purpose. She just happened to mention it." Lara fried the bacon.

"Why are you going there?"

"I promised Chloe I'd teach her a few self-defense moves."

"The gym is never crowded in the winter. People are getting their exercise by skiing. Nobody wants to be inside when there's fresh powder."

"I do," Lara said adamantly.

"If I teach you to ski or snowboard, you'll love it." Lara was adventurous, and she'd take to winter sports if she had a teacher. And he knew just the guy to show her the joy of winter.

"I think I'd rather be sitting by a warm fire doing...something else," she said innocently, but turned and wrapped her arms around his neck.

"I think if I teach you the benefits of staying inside, you'll love it," she parroted him teasingly.

He kissed her, and admitted that she was probably right, especially if she meant staying inside *her*.

"I think I have the basics down, but do you think we could keep practicing?" Chloe asked Lara as she walked at a sedate pace on the treadmill.

Lara was up to a run, but she wasn't out of breath yet. "Sure. We can go over it until I have to leave."

They'd practiced basic self-defense for quite a while before they finished and Lara jumped on the treadmill to do her daily routine. She'd seen a few more bruises on Chloe, and her alarm bells went off pretty damn loud. "Chloe, is James hurting you?" She had to ask. Her conscience wouldn't allow her to stay silent.

Chloe looked straight ahead as she answered. "No. Of course not. The martial arts thing was an accident. He got impatient and he's under a lot of stress right now."

"You have new bruises," Lara argued.

"I'm a klutz," Chloe said hastily. "I trip a lot and do some stupid things. I bruise easily."

She knew she was putting Tate's sister on the defensive, so she answered simply. "If you ever need to talk, I'm here to listen." Sometimes it was easier to talk to a woman than a man.

It hadn't escaped Lara's notice that Chloe had never really called on James when she'd needed him, and during this family crisis it would be nice if he was around to reassure her.

"Thanks," Chloe answered casually. "But I'm good. Every relationship hits some bumpy areas, I think." She paused. "God, do you torture yourself like that every day?"

Lara thought that maybe most relationships did have ups and downs, but she was afraid that Chloe was hitting mountains instead of bumps in her relationship. "Yep. I have no choice but to work out every day. I have to be in good condition for my job, and I like to eat."

"Me too," Chloe answered with a sigh. "But I gain weight if I even smell chocolate or something fattening."

"You're not fat, Chloe," Lara told her sternly, angry that some man had made her feel unattractive when she was actually gorgeous.

"James doesn't really like curvy women."

"Then dump him and find somebody who does," Lara said angrily. "What about that handsome cowboy you were with the other night?"

"Gabe?" Chloe blushed. "He's a billionaire cowboy, and just a friend of the family, mostly a friend of Blake's. And we don't even get along most of the time."

"I think he likes you," Lara countered, decreasing her speed to wind down her run.

"He doesn't. He just likes to joke around. I don't like it."

Lara had a feeling Chloe didn't like it because she didn't believe Gabe when he shot her a compliment. "He looked pretty concerned when Marcus got arrested and Tate got injured."

"He was nice," Chloe admitted as she stopped her treadmill to get off. "But it didn't last very long." Looking uncomfortable, Chloe changed the subject. "Do you care about Tate?"

Lara felt a little uncomfortable as she slowed down to a walk, not liking it when she was on the hot seat. "I do. He helped me out a lot. He's a very brave man, and I admire him a great deal." *And he's so damn hot that I want to do him every minute of the day.* She decided not to share that information with Tate's sister.

Chloe rolled her eyes at Lara. "You know what I mean. Do you have the hots for him?"

Lara flushed. "He's attractive, but I barely know him." Okay, maybe she *did* know Tate intimately, but it hadn't been for very long.

"He's been so detached and lonely since his accident. That's one of the reasons why I wanted him to adopt Shep."

"Tate adores that puppy," Lara told Chloe as she stopped walking and got off the treadmill. "Don't let him tell you anything different."

Chloe smiled at her. "I know he does. He grumbles and complains about Shep, but I couldn't pry that pup away from him now even if I wanted to." Chloe sat down in a chair by the treadmills.

Tate had been right: the gym was empty and she and Chloe had the whole place to themselves.

"He's torn up about Marcus even if he doesn't show it, you know," Chloe said sadly. "I guess we all are. Mom still refuses to believe Marcus is even guilty of anything illegal."

Guilt swamped Lara hard and fast. "I'm so sorry, Chloe."

Chloe looked up at Lara. "You have no reason to be sorry. You were doing your job."

God, Chloe sounded so much like Tate. "Thanks." Lara picked up a towel to dry off her sweat-soaked face.

Both women gathered up their bags to go shower.

"So do you have a boyfriend back in Washington?" Chloe asked slyly.

"No. I haven't had a boyfriend in years."

"What happened to him?" Chloe asked curiously.

"He cheated on me." Funny, but Lara didn't even think about him or his actions anymore. Maybe because he wasn't worth the time or effort it took to get angry about it. The cheating boyfriend had been humiliating, but he had never really touched her emotions like Tate did.

"That sucks. You know, Tate's very loyal once a person has gained his affection."

Lara smiled at Tate's crafty sister. "No matchmaking," she told Chloe with a smile. "Tate lives in Colorado. I live in Washington DC. That presents some very interesting geographical issues."

Chloe shrugged. "He's a pilot."

"Like I said, we barely know each other," Lara said lightly and moved toward the locker room.

"You have to admit, he's a handsome badass," Chloe said proudly.

Thinking about the way Tate did everything, including the way he disarmed three men at one time and shot her attacker, she had to answer, "Agreed." Tate being handsome was an understatement. He was absolutely breathtaking, especially when he was naked, but she kept that information to herself.

She couldn't stay here in Colorado, even if Tate wanted to continue their relationship for a while. She had a life, a career in Washington. She didn't want Chloe even thinking in that direction. "I'm hoping we can all keep in touch," she added, trying to make it sound like leaving Tate would be no big deal.

"Oh, I think we will," Chloe said with a mysterious grin as she walked beside her. "How long are you staying?"

"At least another week," Lara answered, not quite sure how long her boss would let her stay here. But she should be good for at least one more week before he started to hound her to come back to work.

Chloe nodded. "That should be long enough." The pretty brunette entered the locker room.

Lara shook her head, not quite sure what Chloe meant, and followed Tate's sister through the door.

Chapter 12

"That was one of the most terrifying experiences of my life, and I'm an FBI agent," Lara mumbled teasingly as Tate landed his helicopter on the landing pad back on Colter land. Tate Colter piloted a helicopter just like he drove a snowmobile: crazy fast, with his main objective being speed.

"I'll have you know that I'm one of the best helicopter pilots in the world," he answered arrogantly, as if he were offended, as he shut down the helicopter. "I told you I'd get you to Denver and back fast."

"How long have you been flying?" she asked curiously as she put away her headset. Lara had ridden in plenty of helicopters, and there was no doubt Tate Colter was good. He piloted with so much confidence that no matter how crazy he was, she hadn't really had a moment of fear. But it was fun giving him hell about his take-no-prisoners way of doing things.

"Since not long after I could legally drive," he answered, still sounding disgruntled. "I got my pilot's license the next year."

"What else do you fly?"

He shot her a grin. "Anything that moves through the air, baby."

"You don't have a pilot? You fly everything yourself?"

"Yep. I'm a hell of a lot more comfortable being in control."

"Damn. I guess that ruins my chances of joining the mile-high club," she replied jokingly, making sure her voice sounded disappointed as she unbuckled herself from the passenger seat.

Tate moved so quickly that he was almost a blur as he hopped over the front seat to land on the back bench seat so fast that Lara barely saw him go. "Come back here. I'll be more than happy to induct you," he said huskily.

She turned to look at him as he lounged against the back seat, his hand folded over his abdomen, and waited.

"We aren't in the air," she said breathlessly. Her eyes roamed hungrily over Tate. Her blood heated at the thought of straddling him right here and now and taking what she wanted. She couldn't care less about the mile-high club. But she sure as hell wanted *him*. Constantly. Desperately. Almost painfully.

"I think the rules say that you have to have sex in an aircraft while at altitude. We're already elevated here in the mountains, more than a mile high, and we're definitely in an aircraft. Technically I'd say we're good," he replied enthusiastically. "Come here or I'll come and get you. I've needed you all damn day, Lara. I don't want to wait any longer."

Lara sighed. "We can't do this out here." She looked around the airstrip through the window, the portion Marcus used still closed off for investigation. She didn't see anyone around, and Tate had landed on the opposite end of the little airport. Still, it was risky. "People could be coming and going."

"I know two people who are definitely going to be coming," he rasped. He folded his arms across his chest. "Come to me. I dare you. Take what you want." He threw down the challenge intentionally, his eyes heated and beckoning her to come to him.

Dammit. He knows how much I want him, and he's absolutely certain that I won't back down from a dare from him.

She bit her lip, trying to get her undeniable need under control. Tate liked to test her, push her boundaries, but he didn't realize that when it came to him, her boundaries were getting pretty damn wide.

"What do *you* want?" she asked him in a sultry tone. She knelt on the passenger seat and pulled the sweater she wore over her head. She would play his game, and she'd relish it because he wanted her just as much as she wanted him.

"Don't play with me right now, baby," he growled as he pulled his shirt over his head and dropped it on the floor of the helicopter.

He kept her eyes locked with his as she shimmied out of her jeans and panties awkwardly, and then unhooked her bra and shucked it, too. She shivered as the air wafted over her bare skin, her body now completely naked. "Who says I'm playing?" She lifted a brow at him, loving the surprised look on his face. She knew he hadn't really expected her to strip in his helicopter and call him on his dare.

Her eyes roamed over the visible erection that was trying to burst the zipper of his jeans. His gray long-sleeved shirt hugged his muscular arms and chest; the color perfectly matched his eyes.

"Jesus, Lara. You *are* going to kill me." He groaned and held his arms out to her.

Clambering over the controls and the seat, she literally fell on top of him and straddled him. He closed his arms around her immediately, snaked a hand behind her neck and brought her body flush against him. He breathed deeply and nuzzled against her neck. "Screw the mile high. I'll take you as high as you want to go," he commented sharply, his warm breath on her neck. "Your scent makes me want to drown in you." He nipped her skin and then laved over it. "Your taste makes me want to devour you." He reached between their bodies and ran a finger over her drenched core. "And *this* makes me want to fuck you until you scream." His mouth closed over one of her hardened nipples.

Lara leaned back. Tate would never let her fall; she trusted him completely. "I want you, Tate. Please." She ran her hands over his powerful chest, loving the feel of his hot skin beneath her fingers. When she lifted herself to her knees, she gave him space to unzip his pants and lower them to let his engorged cock escape. "Don't you ever wear underwear?" she moaned as she felt the silken steel of him against her fiery sex.

"Hardly ever since the day I met you."

She stifled a laugh at his serious tone. "So you're always ready?" She lowered herself down, shivering as she slid her pussy along the wide, hard shaft of his cock.

"I'm always hopeful," he corrected as he placed his hands on her hips. "Do you want to grant the wish of an optimistic man?"

Tate's eagerness emboldened her. The way he sounded, the way he talked to her made her feel as if she were a goddess, as though he was lucky to have her. She felt like the most desirable woman on earth. Probably because she thought Tate was the hottest man on the planet, and he wanted her.

"I can't grant wishes," she told him teasingly as she grasped his cock and placed it against her sheath. "I'm not magical."

"To me you are," Tate grunted as he guided her down onto him. "Ride me, Lara. Take what you want, whatever you need from me."

Her heart raced as she looked down into his tumultuous eyes, molten with desire and one of the most beautiful things she'd ever seen. Her breath caught as he urged her all the way down, completely seating himself inside her.

"I'm feeling very needy." She rocked her hips.

"Thank fuck," he groaned. He grasped her ass and rocked her against him again.

Lara started to move, using her bent legs for leverage and balance, and wrapped her arms around Tate's shoulders. She closed her eyes; she absorbed his essence, let her body undulate with his erotically, satisfyingly, and let him fill her senses completely.

They moved together as one, and Lara savored the slow build of heat, the intimacy of having him inside her, the feel of his hand running up and down her back soothingly. This was no race to the finish line. The urgency was there, but it was as if neither one of them wanted it to end.

Her hands speared into his hair; she brought her mouth down to his and tangled their tongues together in a sensual, intimate dance while she moved harder, faster.

He groaned into her mouth. Tate stroked her ass, finally grasping it as though he had snapped, and lifted his hips to intensify the strength of his entry inside her, fucking her as though he needed her, had to possess her completely.

"Mine," he ground out as Lara lifted her mouth from his. "You're mine, baby. I'll never let you go."

His dominant words triggered her climax; her body echoed his declaration as she ground against him, trying to claim him as her own with her body.

She wanted.

She needed.

She was desperate.

She was…his.

"Oh, God. Tate." She panted as ripples became massive waves that crashed over her. She clung to him, threw her head back and screamed as her orgasm tore through her body. She felt Tate shudder against her and follow her over the edge with a groan of ecstasy.

He held her against him covetously, one arm around her waist and the other on her ass. "That was a hell of a lot more than a mile high."

Lara smiled as she held his head against her breasts. "Definitely," she agreed, still in a daze, her body limp against his. Still flying above the clouds, Lara wondered whether she'd ever come down again.

"My boss sent me a text. He wants me back in DC soon. We're shorthanded and he needs me back to work," Lara told Tate quietly as they ate dinner together later that evening. "I was hoping I'd have more time, but he's insistent."

Tate nearly choked on his pasta as he inhaled to protest. He coughed and took a sip of his beer, looking at her before he spoke. "Don't go back."

Jesus. I can't stand the thought of her leaving. The house would be empty without her. I'll be empty without her.

She looked up at him and placed her fork on her plate. "You know I have to go back home. I have a career, and so do you. I don't know what you're still doing with the government, but I know you work a lot with the fire equipment company, developing new products. We both have our own very different lives."

"I don't travel much anymore, and I work with research and development in Denver for Colter Fire Equipment. I'm not there every day. I have professionals doing that job. I just give my input, and try to come up with new ideas."

Shep whined at Lara's feet, as though he knew what they were discussing. Hell, even his damn dog adored her. She couldn't leave.

"I take my career seriously, Tate. I'm not a billionaire. My parents weren't exactly prepared to die at such a young age. I got my degree from my inheritance, but I couldn't go beyond a bachelor's degree." She took a sip of the white wine that she loved she'd found in his wine cellar.

Tate had already put in an order for several cases of the same wine.

"Is that why you joined the FBI?" he asked her huskily.

"Yes and no. I wanted to do something I was passionate about. Obviously I'm passionate about terrorism. Working for the FBI was a reasonable choice."

"What else were you passionate about?"

"I got my degree in psychology. At one time, I wanted to be a counselor or a psychologist," she admitted, her voice wistful.

"So do it. Stay here and finish school. Hell, maybe you could fix me." Lord knew everybody told him he was crazy.

She smiled at him. "There's not a thing I would want to change. Okay, maybe the cooking thing. But you're rich. You don't need to cook." She picked up her fork again and twirled the pasta around the utensil. "I was hoping to work with abused women to get them out of the cycle of abuse."

"Why?" Tate was fascinated now.

"I told you that I went to live with my aunt after my parents died. My uncle was abusive," she answered in a sad voice.

"Did he hurt you?" Tate clenched his fist around the beer he held.

Lara shook her head. "No. But he hurt my aunt. I begged her to leave him, but he always came back and told her he was sorry, that he'd never do it again. Unfortunately, she couldn't get out of the cycle. I only had to stay there for a little over a year to finish high school before I left for college, and he never touched me. But I wanted to get her out. I couldn't."

The regret and sadness in Lara's eyes made Tate's chest ache. "Where is she now?"

"She passed away a few years ago of cancer."

"I'm sorry, baby." She was damn alone in the world. All Tate wanted to do was hold her, be her confidante when she needed someone. "What's your life like in Washington?"

"Mostly work." She shrugged. "You know what it's like to live for your job. I have a small apartment, my friends at the department. I'm content for now. I want to build up my savings and go back to school eventually. The shelf life of an agent isn't all that long."

Tate knew that between burnout and age, being a field agent could be a relatively short career. Agents had to be in top physical condition, and it was a demanding job. "Leave now. Stay with me and go back to school. You won't have to work, Lara."

She chewed and swallowed before she answered. "Not happening. I'm not sponging off a friend, even if he is a billionaire."

"I'm more than your friend," he rumbled irritably. "I'm one of the founders of a new charitable organization to help abused women. You could work there. Do what you really want to do."

Her face registered surprise. "You mean the new one being started up by those billionaire brothers in Florida?"

Tate nodded. "Lots of billionaires, and not just in Florida. The Hudsons and the Harrisons are founding members, and so am I. My brothers are getting involved now, too. And Grady Sinclair in Maine."

"Wow. That's a lot of firepower."

Tate smirked, amused by the way Lara measured everything by guns and law enforcement. "You could be part of it. Kade Harrison's wife was abused, and she's determined to do everything she can to help battered women get out of their situations. She'd be happy to have somebody trained to work with."

He saw a flash of longing in Lara's eyes before she slowly shook her head. "I'd still need more schooling, and I'm not ready to leave my job right now. But I might take you up on your offer in the future."

Dammit. She was stubborn. Tate didn't think it was a situation where she didn't want to leave her job at the FBI, but pure dogged independence. He admired that and hated it at the same time. "When were you thinking about going back?" It ate at him to even think about her leaving.

"Tuesday."

It was Friday. Dammit. He only had three more days to convince her to stay. He got up to take his dishes to the kitchen, racking his brain for any way to entice her to stay with him. Any other solution was unacceptable. "I'll fly you back. I'd like to see Blake. I talked to him yesterday, but he isn't exactly very forthcoming with information. I think it would be better if I talked to him in person."

Lara picked up her own dishes and brought them into the kitchen; she nodded in response.

Honestly, he didn't plan to take her anywhere at all except to bed, but he'd deal with the travel situation when and if it happened. Right now, he had to find a way to keep her with him.

I'm a goddamn Colter, and Colters never quit, never give up.

He came from a stubborn lineage, men who never stopped trying. It was the reason they were all so wealthy today. Every Colter ancestor had been tenacious—some of them downright cantankerous. But they had never stopped trying to start new businesses, to keep progressing.

Tate hadn't survived years of nearly suicidal missions only to lose the only woman he'd ever wanted. *Not. Happening.* Lara was about to find out just how ornery and insistent he could really be.

Chapter 13

S unday afternoon, Lara stood at the picture window of Tate's home, and watched him walk Shep. She smiled as she saw his lips move; he was talking to the puppy, probably telling the dog how unreasonable she was being.

Tate had spent all day yesterday trying to sell her on the merits of staying in Colorado. After she'd finished with an early-morning session with Chloe at the gym, he'd taken her skiing. By the end of the day, her ass had been bruised and battered, but she'd been able to stay on her skis in an upright position down the beginner slopes. And it had been fun, challenging, and they'd laughed a lot, something she didn't do a whole lot of in her life up until she'd met Tate.

He'd flown her to Denver for dinner last night, wining and dining her, complete with roses and champagne. He'd been sweet and seductive, bringing her home and taking her straight to bed, where he'd rocked her world all over again.

If he was trying to sell her on Colorado and the billionaire lifestyle, she definitely had no arguments. Tate had an incredible family, a gorgeous home, and she already loved Colorado. It was different from living in Washington, but in a good way. It was peaceful, and Rocky Springs was a wonderful small town.

The problem was…she was in love with Tate Colter.

She sighed as she propped her hip against the window, and watched him patiently wait for Shep to find a place to pee. It wasn't that she didn't want to stay; she couldn't stay. Her heart already felt lacerated and painful. Being around Tate every day and not blurting out exactly how she felt would be impossible.

He wanted her to stay, but that didn't mean he loved her. Tate didn't seem ready to love, and she couldn't stand the agony of loving somebody as much as she loved him and not have the emotions reciprocated.

It's not his fault that he doesn't feel the same way.

Lara didn't blame him. Maybe he wasn't ready, or maybe she just wasn't his forever woman. She didn't regret the time she had spent with him. He'd…changed her somehow, made her feel like a woman. Now that he'd opened a new world to her, she couldn't go back. And she couldn't ignore the fact that her heart was wide open to him, and he didn't want it.

Staying would just be a Band-Aid to her open wound. It might feel better for a time, but in the end she'd be devastated. She'd have to rip off the Band-Aid and let her heart heal—if that was even possible. Somehow, Lara didn't think she was going to get over Tate Colter anytime soon. She'd never met a man like him, and she knew plenty of guys. He was…unique.

She turned away from the window; her eyes flooded with tears. As she sat down at the table, she swiped them away angrily. The last thing she needed was for Tate to see her crying. He had enough to deal with in his family right now. He didn't need a pathetic, weepy woman who loved him so much that she could hardly breathe when she thought about leaving him.

At dinner the night before, she'd asked Tate whether he wanted to talk about Marcus. She knew he was torn up inside, but he didn't want to speak about it. He said it was too soon, and he had to sort out his feelings. He was in denial, and Lara knew Marcus's betrayal would eventually crash down on him. She wanted to help him, but she didn't want to push if he wasn't ready to talk.

Maybe he'll call me when he's ready to talk.

One thing was for certain: she'd talk to him about it even if hearing his voice from so far away nearly killed her. He'd need someone to listen when he finally accepted what Marcus had done.

Tate came into the house just then, leaving his boots on the porch and letting Shep off the leash. He took off his jacket and hat; his hair had that spiky style that made her want to jump him. Okay, she *always* wanted to jump him, but it made the urge even stronger. He looked particularly attractive today in a pair of faded jeans and a tan fisherman's sweater.

Shep bounded toward her, wiggling at her feet and trying to crawl up the leg of her jeans. She picked him up with a happy laugh and snuggled him against the cotton of her long-sleeved turtleneck. "Why do you always come to me when you're cold?" She shivered as the dog's tiny, cold body huddled against her.

"Because you're so hot. He knows how to get warm. Smart dog," Tate said with a naughty smirk.

She rolled her eyes at Tate, but she secretly loved it when he inferred that she was attractive. A man who actually treated her as if she was a desirable woman was still a novelty for her, and she ate it up as though it was chocolate.

Lara sneaked a peek at Tate's perfect, tight ass while he walked into the kitchen to get Shep's food. The dog leaped off her lap the moment Tate filled the puppy's bowl. "Abandoned for food," she grumbled good-naturedly.

Tate looked at her from across the room, his eyes heated. "I guess he isn't always smart. I'd give up the food to be cuddled up to you in a heartbeat."

She shot him back a silly grin. "I'm honored."

Lara startled as the doorbell rang.

"I'll grab it. It's probably your mom and Chloe," Lara said as she hopped up, always glad to see Aileen and Chloe. She hadn't expected to see them today because she and Tate visited with them at the resort yesterday morning after she and Chloe were done in the gym.

She opened the door with a smile, a happy expression that faded to confusion as she saw a completely different face than the ones she had expected. "Blake? I thought you were still in Washington."

The expression on Tate's brother's face was grim, and he was minus his cowboy hat today. He was dressed in a dark custom suit and a dark wool winter jacket.

"May I come in?" he asked politely.

Lara opened the door and let him step inside.

"What the fuck are you doing here, Marcus?" Tate's angry voice sounded from behind Lara.

Marcus? This was Marcus?

"Are you sure?" she asked Tate sharply as she stepped back from the man who had just entered and drew her gun from the holster at her back. She was certain Tate was correct. It seemed impossible, but he recognized his own brothers.

"Yeah, I'm sure," Tate answered furiously.

Lara stepped far enough away from Marcus that he couldn't take her weapon and trained it on him. "You better explain damn fast before I shoot you." How in the hell had he escaped from prison and made it all the way here to Colorado? And why was he dressed as if he were going to the office?

Marcus's brows narrowed. "Put the gun down. I'm here to talk. I need to talk to Tate."

"Talk? You take one step toward him, and I'll kill you. How did you get out of jail?" she repeated, her aim steady.

"I was released legally," Marcus replied calmly.

"Bullshit," Tate exploded as he strode toward Marcus and grasped him by the collar of his jacket. "They don't release terrorists from prison. Try again."

"Tate, you're blocking me. Move," Lara demanded, antsy because Tate was now in her sights.

Marcus shrugged off Tate's hold. "Just listen to me. I am not a terrorist. I work for the CIA." He flipped open a leather holder and held up an ID.

Tate ripped it from his hand and scrutinized it thoroughly. "It looks legit," he told Lara hoarsely.

She moved forward and took it from his hand, recognizing the identification. If it was fake, he had a damn good forger. And what would be the point?

Marcus held out the phone he held in his other hand. "The number for the CIA is in my phone. Call the director. Verify the number and call through the central number, then ask for him. He's expecting your call."

Lara dropped his ID on the table, but kept her eyes on Marcus as Tate did exactly as Marcus instructed. He verified the number on his laptop before he called it. She heard Tate talking, but her attention was focused on his brother.

He looked different today, his eyes far from emotionless. Marcus looked tired, and his Colter gray eyes shone with sadness and remorse.

Good Lord...was it actually possible that Marcus was telling the truth? Please. Please. Let it be true. It would mean so much to Tate if Marcus was actually a good guy. But if he was, what the hell was he doing with all of those explosives?

Tate ended his conversation, clicked off the cell phone and handed it back to Marcus. "Put the gun away, Lara," Tate told her flatly. "He's telling the truth."

What. The. Hell.

Lara holstered her gun, still confused. "How? Why?"

Marcus inclined his head to her. "Thank you for not shooting me."

"Thank Tate. I wanted to shoot you," she mumbled irritably. After the hell he'd put Tate through, she'd wanted to hurt Marcus. Bad.

Marcus chuckled. "I'm sure you did and probably still do." He looked at Tate. "You've certainly found yourself a loyal woman."

"She's fucking amazing," Tate corrected. "Are you planning on telling me what the hell is going on? Does everyone else know?" He motioned to the table.

They all sat down, and Lara found it surreal that she was actually looking across the table at a man who she'd thought was a terrorist only a short time ago.

Marcus started to talk. "Blake has known since he came to Washington and I could speak with him in person. I met with Zane in Denver before I got here, and I just came from a long discussion with Chloe and Mom."

"So I'm the last to know," Tate grumbled.

"I knew you were going to be the hardest one to tell," Marcus said soberly. "I got you injured, Tate. And Lara was humiliated and hurt as well. I'm sorry."

"It's part of my job," Lara answered quietly. "Can you explain how the FBI didn't know about you?"

Marcus nodded. "Not very many people knew, and I'm not surprised that they put an FBI counter-terrorist team on this case. I expected it. My trail wasn't exactly discreet and it wasn't meant to be. But it was top secret, and we didn't want any information leaked. The lowest-ranked person at the CIA who knew was the deputy director of NCS, and the director of the FBI was informed but not allowed to share the information."

"What was your mission?" Tate asked gruffly.

Marcus grimaced. "It was actually something I got involved in inadvertently. This group was fairly sophisticated, and they had money. They were posing as legitimate and respected businessmen. I heard an exchange that I'm sure I wasn't supposed to understand. It was being discussed in Arabic at a business function."

"You speak a lot of languages," Lara mused.

Marcus shrugged. "I deal with a lot of countries, and I have a knack for picking up languages."

"So then what?" Tate prompted.

"I approached the CIA with the information."

"How long have you been helping the CIA?"

"Awhile," Marcus admitted reluctantly. "I travel and I pick up limited information to help them out. I've assisted with gathering information for them in the past, but nothing on quite the same scale as this particular operation. They asked me if I could possibly get close to these men, try to infiltrate the group somehow. It wasn't easy. I'm American and they didn't trust me. It took me two years to finally convince them that all I wanted was money, and that I didn't care about their cause. They didn't want me to. They just needed an American cover to buy the explosives so it didn't rouse as much suspicion. Since we're a prominent family, they decided to take the risk. The plan was to get all the explosives together and we'd do the final deal. I'd be given payment and they'd fly out their explosives. What you interrupted was the check of the final shipment before we made our transaction. Nothing was supposed to happen that day. The director was planning on getting together a special team, including the FBI, for the final bust. I wanted to make sure my family was gone, away from the area before anything happened." Marcus paused for a moment before continuing, "I should have never used the airstrip, or Rocky Springs."

"You didn't have much of a choice. It's a private airport. Where else could you have arranged this?" Lara said quietly, knowing he had the perfect bait for the terrorists because he did have a private airport and the Colters were a highly respected family.

"It endangered my family," Marcus replied bleakly.

"Normally, it wouldn't have," Tate said honestly. "The airstrip is a safe distance away from our homes and the resort. Lara and I being there was accidental. I wanted to prove to her that you weren't involved so she'd stop trying to attract your attention."

Marcus smiled and glanced at Lara. "Oh, she would have attracted my attention. But I probably would have guessed that she was a fed."

"You never would have known," Lara said defensively. "I'm damn good at my job."

Marcus's smile grew broader. "And I'm highly connected." He looked at Tate. "Did you mark her as a fed?"

"Yeah. But only because I checked her out for personal information. I didn't really suspect she was FBI. I just knew she wasn't our average type of guest at the resort."

"I've checked out everyone who even speaks to me for the last two years. I had no doubt the FBI were looking, but we weren't ready to form a team. We needed the evidence first," Marcus explained.

"Why did you let the team arrest you?" Lara asked curiously.

"All of the terrorists weren't there. We had to round up the rest of the group. They would have bolted immediately if they knew I was involved with the CIA. I had to wait until the remaining group was in custody, and we needed to set a trap. If I would have exposed myself then, it would have made it more difficult for me to assist in luring the rest of the group to an arrest area," Marcus informed her. "I was damn glad you had backup, Agent Bailey. I went to the storage room to try to get an emergency text to the director while the terrorists were busy checking the merchandise, but they weren't going to make it in time. I was already trying to think of an alternate plan."

"You didn't tell them I was your brother," Tate remarked. "I don't understand Arabic nearly as well as you do, but it sounded like you were telling them that we were police."

Marcus nodded. "There was no way I wanted them to know we were related. They're paranoid and crazy. It was better to let them think we'd been discovered by the local authorities and needed to move quicker. I was going to try to get them to provide the money so that they could start transporting the goods while I held you two to give them time to escape. It would have bought us some time, but I'm not certain they would have agreed, and I didn't know how quickly law enforcement would be sent. Believe me...I was more than happy to be arrested along with everybody else by the FBI. I was just glad they were in custody, and Agent Bailey had the forethought to bring in backup. I was worried about you bleeding to death on me."

"Please call me Lara. And I didn't trust you like Tate did."

"I'm glad." Marcus shot Lara a grateful look.

"Nothing has leaked to the media yet," Tate observed.

Marcus shook his head. "With any luck, it won't. We kept a pretty tight lid on all of this. The only civilians who know are Gabe and my family, and Gabe already knows the real truth now. He says he won't tell anyone, and I believe him. The hospital had no idea what happened to you, Tate. They reported the stabbing, but the report went to the police, and they aren't talking. I'd really prefer this not turn into gossip, and as few people as possible know that I work with the CIA."

"That makes sense if you ever want to function as an operative again," Lara agreed.

"I can't believe my brother is a damn spy," Tate grumbled. "Jesus, you're likely to get yourself killed by playing James Bond."

Marcus gave Tate a reproving stare. "Like you can talk? What I do is a hell of a lot safer than any of your past missions." Marcus turned to Lara. "And what was your objective here at the resort?"

"To get close to you and seduce you into talking. All we knew was that you were purchasing and flying large amounts of explosives. It was an investigative assignment."

"Nice," Marcus said as smooth as silk. His eyes moved over her nonchalantly. "Exactly how much seduction would that have involved?" he questioned.

"None," Tate growled. "She's off-limits."

Marcus grinned. "Not anymore. We're both on the same side."

"I really regretted punching you in the face. Don't make me do it again," Tate warned in a menacing voice.

"Feeling a little possessive, little brother?" Marcus sounded amused.

"Yes," Tate affirmed.

"And how does that work out for you, Lara?" Marcus asked.

It's hot. So damn hot that I want to tackle Tate and screw him until I can't breathe.

"I can handle him," Lara told Marcus with a smile.

"Somehow, I'm pretty certain you can," Marcus said as he rose. "I have to take care of some details, but we'll talk more later. I just wanted you both to know that I'm sorry. You have no idea how hard it was not to reveal who I was. But I think it probably would have gotten us all dead. I was terrified that Tate was going to bleed to death. I came pretty close to blowing my cover anyway."

Lara was pretty certain Marcus was right. He'd handled things well, considering he was concerned for his younger brother. Even if she hadn't seen through Marcus's disguise before, she could see his concern and regret now.

She and Tate rose to see Marcus out. On instinct, she grasped Marcus's arm. He turned to her questioningly.

"Tate always believed in you. Even when I presented the damning evidence, he laughed in my face. He never believed you were guilty," she told Marcus urgently, wanting to make sure neither one of the brothers ended up resentful.

"I know." Marcus patted her hand. "I'm sorry, little brother," he told Tate sincerely.

Lara moved her hand from Marcus's arm and she watched as two sets of gray Colter eyes clashed in understanding. Marcus reached out and grabbed Tate up in a bear hug. Tate wrapped his clenched fists around Marcus's body; the two of them pounded each other on the back. Both men were about the same size, and Lara wondered whether they'd hurt each other in their manly show of affection.

"I'm so fucking glad you're safe," Tate told him as the two men broke apart, both of them still slapping each other on the back.

"I'm glad both of you are okay." Marcus looked back and forth at Tate and Lara.

Lara moved forward and pulled Marcus into a hug. "Thank you."

Those two words covered so many things:

Thank you for being innocent so Tate won't hurt anymore.

Thank you for being a rich guy and still caring enough to help stop terrorists.

Thank you for caring about a lowly FBI agent who was just doing her job.

Thank you for loving your younger brother because I love him, too.

Marcus didn't hesitate to hug her back before he let her go. Lara grabbed his ID that she had dropped on the table and handed it back to him.

His hand still on the door, Marcus turned to her with a mischievous smile that suddenly reminded her very much of Tate. "You know, I might have let you seduce me. But I never would have talked," he said flirtatiously, leaning in close to her so Tate couldn't hear him.

She rolled her eyes at his arrogant words and whispered in his ear, "You would have been singing like a bird, Colter."

Marcus just laughed as he exited and closed the door behind him.

"Was he flirting with you?" Tate asked gruffly as he stared at the closed door with a frown.

"He was being a smart ass," Lara admitted. "It seems to be something all of you Colter brothers excel at."

"My brother isn't a terrorist," Tate said quietly.

"I know." She lifted her hand to stroke his whiskered jaw.

"My brother isn't a terrorist!" he whooped, lifted her by the waist, and swung her around until he reached the living room.

Lara's heart soared at the joy in Tate's voice. Tears of happiness flowed down her face. "I know."

"He's a damn CIA operative. Marcus is a spy." Tate collapsed on the couch, pulling her down with him, and laughed. He reached out and hugged her against him. His voice cracked with emotion as he said emphatically, "Thank fuck!"

Lara hugged him back, rocking him against her, sharing his joy as tears continued to flow down her face: tears of relief for Tate and the entire Colter family. They'd be whole again, unbroken because Marcus was everything Tate had always said he was.

He held her for over an hour, neither of them saying much of anything.

Their emotions spent, they fell asleep in each other's arms. Tate woke up a few hours later and carried her gently into the bedroom with him.

Chapter 14

Lara's heart squeezed tightly in her chest as she packed the next morning. The weather forecast wasn't good for Tuesday, so she was outbound later tonight before the storm moved in. Her boss had made her reservations out of Denver, and she'd catch that flight. It would be so much easier than trying to say good-bye to Tate in Washington.

One day less. Does it matter?

Right now, it felt as if it mattered a great deal. She wanted that extra day, resented having to give him up any sooner than tomorrow.

"What are you doing?" Tate sounded confused as he came into the bedroom.

"There's a storm moving in. I'm going to have to leave tonight. The department made me a reservation on a commercial flight. I have to be on it." She couldn't look at him. If she did, she'd lose it.

"You can't go today. We're supposed to have until tomorrow." Tate's voice sounded desperate.

"I don't have a choice." Lara folded a pair of jeans and dropped them into her suitcase.

Please don't let him touch me. If he does, I'll give in. I'll probably beg, plead, ask him if I can stay with him, even if it's not forever.

I can't do that. I can't give up the job I've worked so hard at for a longer fling.

"Fine. I'll fly you to Denver," he said harshly.

She nodded, having no reason to object. She'd have to get there somehow. "I'd like to stop and say good-bye to your mom and Chloe."

He moved up behind her, his voice pleading, "Lara, please stay."

"I can't," she replied firmly. Tears clouded her vision.

He moved his hands and stepped back. "I can't make you want me, I guess."

Don't say anything. Don't tell him how desperately you want him, how lonely you'll be without him. It will just prolong the inevitable and it will hurt even more.

She bit her lip. Hard. Finally, he stalked out of the room and left her alone.

Lara let the tears fall, mourning the loss of Tate before she'd even left him.

Tate took Shep outside, his anger and desperation at war with each other. What could he do? He couldn't force her to stay. She wanted her job. He wanted her. They were at an impasse, and there was nothing he could do to make things turn out differently. Truthfully, he didn't want her that way. He wanted her willingly. He wanted a commitment, something that would bind her to him forever.

She didn't ask if I wanted to go live in Washington. She never even asked.

For Lara, he'd do it in a heartbeat. He didn't care where he lived as long as he was with her.

She didn't ask. For her, the relationship is impossible. I just have to admit that she isn't feeling it as much as I am.

Yesterday, he'd been ecstatic because he'd learned Marcus wasn't a criminal. Today, he felt defeated.

Colters don't quit.

Hell, he wouldn't quit if he had any other option.

His cell phone vibrated in his pocket. Because it was one of his oldest friends, Travis Harrison, he answered.

"Yeah."

"Tate?" Travis's voice was solemn.

"It's me."

"You're going to think I'm crazy, but do you know someone named Lara?"

Tate was instantly alert. "Yeah. I know her. I'm crazy about her."

Tate quickly explained that Lara was here and getting ready to fly back to Washington. Briefly, he talked about their whirlwind relationship. "I'm in love with her," he admitted to Travis. "Letting her leave is killing me, Trav."

"Don't let her go," Travis said urgently. "Tate, I had a dream. I haven't had one this vivid for a long time. But I dreamed that you were mourning her death in a plane crash. Wherever she's going, don't let her go on her flight."

Fuck! Tate had learned to take Travis's dream premonitions seriously. One of his dreams had once saved Tate's life, and another the life of Travis's wife, Ally.

"When will it happen?" Tate asked anxiously.

"I don't know, but I never dream of something that vivid that isn't happening soon. If she's flying, don't let her go. I know you think I'm crazy—"

"I don't," Tate interrupted. "I know that what you experience is for real. It saved my life and Ally's."

"Then don't let Lara fly. Not commercially anytime soon," Travis warned morosely. "If you love her, keep her there, even if she doesn't believe me."

Lara might not believe in Travis's dreams, but Tate did. He'd seen proof of the strange phenomena several times. At one time, he hadn't believed it. But he did now. "I'll think of something. She's an FBI agent, so I'm not sure she'll go for me telling her the truth."

"You're in love with an FBI agent?" Travis asked. "Why am I not surprised? Can she kick your ass?"

"No," Tate denied. "But she can put up a damn good fight."

"Good for her. She sounds like your kind of woman."

"She is," Tate agreed. "I've never felt like this before, Trav. How do you live with feeling the way you do about Ally?"

"It's hell, buddy. But you'll get through it. If you love her, and she loves you, it's the most amazing feeling in the world."

Tate shook his head even though Travis couldn't see him. "She doesn't love me."

"Then change her mind," Travis answered gruffly. "If anybody can wear a woman down, it's you. Don't give up. And try telling her that you love her. You're willing to take chances with everything else, including your own life. Take a chance on her."

Tate wanted to, but he was too damn scared that she'd tear his heart out. "She hasn't told me she loves me." And he was pretty certain she didn't if she was willing to just walk away from their relationship.

"Did you tell her?" Travis questioned bluntly.

"Nope."

"Then how do you know how she feels? Talk to her," Travis suggested. "And keep her with you for now."

"I plan on it," Tate answered hoarsely, thinking about the horror of losing Lara completely. He'd never live through it.

"I'll call later and see how things are going," Travis told him, his voice concerned.

"Thanks, Trav. Seriously. I appreciate the warning." Tate knew Travis didn't talk to anybody about his strange talent. But they'd been friends for a long time, so he'd taken that chance.

"Stay safe," Travis rumbled.

"You, too." Tate disconnected. His mind whirled as he stuffed his phone back into his pocket.

Lara would never believe him if he told her that he had a psychic friend. She'd still get on that plane, and she'd die. He felt it in his gut, the same way he knew that Ally would have been dead had Travis not spirited her away during the time of her possible demise.

"Let's go, boy. I've got some planning to do." He pulled on Shep's leash, and urged him back to the house as soon as the puppy had watered the edge of the woods.

He thought as he walked back to the house, finally pulling his phone out of his pocket as he reached the porch. Tate had a plan, but it was a little drastic. Lara would be mad, but it was much preferable to her being dead.

He made the calls.

Lara had cried as she hugged Shep for the last time. She had cried when she said good-bye to Aileen and Chloe, too. Damned if she hadn't felt like a damn leaky bucket all day long.

She sighed as she settled into the passenger seat of the helicopter, looking over at the closed-off portion of the airport.

Obviously, the investigation still wasn't finished and the area was still shut down.

If not for the investigation, Tate and I never would have met.

Try as she might, Lara still couldn't regret meeting Tate and being with him during this stolen time. He'd opened up her eyes to so many things, namely her own sexuality. The problem was, she didn't have any desire to explore that newfound desire with anyone except him.

Tate had been quiet most of the day, telling her he had to go out and take care of some things. It had hurt that he hadn't wanted to spend her last hours in Colorado with her, but it was probably better that way.

They'd fly to Denver, and she'd say a hasty good-bye, never letting him see her tears until she was well away from him.

They lifted off quickly. Lara felt as though her stomach had stayed on the ground while the rest of her body was still in the helicopter. She looked down at the huge pine trees and the open spaces with no people. She could see Blake's ranch in the distance, and it spread out in most directions as far as she could see. The only thing next to Blake's spread was Gabe's home and horse farm.

She rode along in silence, looking at the Colorado scenery for a long time, nervously trying to keep herself occupied. Finally, she looked at their position and where the helicopter was headed.

And it wasn't to Denver.

"Where are we going?" she squeaked as she realized that Tate was actually landing.

"I want to show you something," he answered in a graveled voice.

"I don't have much time to catch my flight." She needed to get there early, and she had lingered for a while with Tate's mom and Chloe.

"That won't be a problem," Tate answered nonchalantly.

"Of course it's a problem. It's listed as being an on-time flight right now. I take off in less than two hours. We have to head to the airport now." She was anxious as he lowered the helicopter into a mass of pine trees. Not that she was worried about him landing safely, but she was concerned about the area in which he landed. They were nowhere near the airport.

"It's not an issue," Tate repeated.

"Why?"

"Because I'm not taking you to the airport," he said in a husky voice in her ear.

Lara looked around frantically, seeing nothing but mountains and trees as they landed.

She pulled off her headphones as Tate shut down the aircraft. "What in the hell are you doing?"

He pulled his headphones off and looked her straight in the eyes. His eyes were dark gray and incredibly intense as he informed her, "I'm detaining you temporarily."

Lara stopped and gaped at him before he hopped out of the helicopter without further explanation.

What the hell was he doing?

She opened the door, turned in the seat and looked around, seeing absolutely nothing but wilderness. The landing pad had been cleared, but everything else was buried in snow.

Tate appeared, lifted her out of the seat, and closed the door behind her after he lowered her to the ground.

Luckily, she wore boots, and they were buried, the snow up to her knees. "Tate, we have to go. My flight—"

"Will be leaving without you," Tate concluded her sentence. "Something is going to happen on that flight. Something bad. You'll be as far away as possible."

She trudged through the snow beside him and he tugged her along. "Do you know something? We have to warn somebody if something is planned—"

"It's not like that," Tate grumbled. "I have a friend who has psychic dreams. He saw me mourning your death in a plane crash. That is one dream I don't want to see in real life. I'm not taking that chance."

Lara could see the back of a cabin ahead. "Your friend has precognition dreams?"

"I know it sounds crazy, but Travis knows. He saved my life once, and he saved the life of his own wife."

She didn't think he was crazy, and she couldn't deny that foresight in dreams was possible, but...

"Precognitive dreams are pretty unpredictable," she told him as they arrived on the back porch of the cabin. "I don't think you're crazy, but I can't live my life because somebody I don't know foresaw my death. It could be many years in the future, or it may never happen." She didn't know his friend, but he could be delusional.

"I know him, and it isn't far into the future. His dreams only come rarely now, and only about people he's close to or family. Travis and I have been buddies for years." Tate unlocked the door with a key left under the mat and pushed it open.

"So kidnapping was the only answer?" She propped her hands on her hips after she entered the door.

"Would you have waited for another flight later?"

"No," she answered him honestly.

"Then yeah...sidetracking you was the only option."

"For exactly how long?" She was angry now. Maybe he thought he was doing the right thing, but she didn't know his friend, and it should have been her choice to risk it or not. There were very few documented cases of true precognitive dreams, and they weren't predictable at all. Lara didn't discount that dream foresight could happen. The power of the human mind was somewhat of a mystery, which was why she'd always been fascinated by psychology. But she would never live her life based on the possibility that she could die some day in the future from a plane crash. It could very well be some kind of coincidence, or just a regular dream.

They both shed their outerwear. The cabin was already warm.

"As long as it takes," Tate answered abruptly as he walked into the cabin.

Lara followed and looked around the small hideaway. The cabin was one enormous room with real log construction and huge log beams along the high ceiling. There was a kitchenette on the other side of the room, a wood burning stove next to her that seemed to be throwing off a whole lot of heat, and rustic and charming furniture. Along one of the walls was a king-sized bed with a comfy looking patchwork quilt, the carved wood frame enormous. It looked like it was probably hand carved.

"Tate, that's not even reasonable. In all likelihood, nothing will happen. People think they have precognitive dreams all the time, and they're just coincidence." She tried to use logic because Tate was the most logical man she'd ever known. It was difficult to hang onto her anger when he was obviously concerned about her. She could see it in his expression.

"Don't you think I know that? But I can't take that chance. Travis has been right too many times," he growled.

"And if nothing happens?"

"I want to stay here for just a little while," Tate admitted.

"For how long?"

"Until I can make you love me," he replied in a guttural tone. His eyes looked at her intensely.

Lara's heart clenched and beat at a rapid pace; a lump formed in her throat. She swallowed hard and choked out, "Why?"

"I want you to love me as much as I love you." He paced the enormous room, circumventing the chairs in the living room area as he walked back and forth restlessly across the cabin. "Honestly,

I doubt that's even possible because I love you so damn much that I can't fucking think rationally anymore. You're my obsession. My thoughts all focused on you almost from the day we met. I'm scared you'll get hurt, that something will happen to you, and I'm damn terrified that once you leave, I'll lose my sanity."

Lara choked back a sob as she watched Tate move like a caged lion. His agitation and vulnerability brought her to her knees.

He loves me.

Not only did he love her, but he loved her every bit as much as she loved him. Tears trickled down her cheeks as she watched his powerful body, now dressed in only a pair of jeans and a forest green sweater, move unceasingly. His expression was grim, and he speared an agitated hand through his already spiked hair.

Finally, he stopped right in front of her. "Tell me what I have to do and I'll do it," he grunted as his nostrils flared. His eyes were molten and swirled with a dozen emotions, all of them powerful and intense. "No limits."

Lara felt her nipples harden and her pussy spasm painfully. The wildness in Tate aroused her unbearably; his vulnerability broke her heart. "You don't have to do anything," she confessed.

"No hope for me?" he asked sharply. His eyes sparked, and then changed to a silver sorrow.

Lara's heart skipped a beat. "No hope for me either," she whispered huskily. "I think I fell for you from the moment you saved those waffles for me at the buffet," she told him lightly. "And I've just kept falling until I know I can't escape."

Luckily, now that she knew he loved her, she didn't want to escape. She just wanted to wallow in Tate.

"You love me?" he asked incredulously.

"So much it hurts," she answered with a sob, swiping at her tears.

Tate wrapped his muscular arms around her body, squeezing her so hard against him that Lara could hardly breathe, but she didn't care. Her arms snaked around his neck and she inhaled the scent of him, drowning in her love for him.

"Why didn't you tell me, baby? Jesus, I love you so damn much," he said in a harsh tone.

"I was afraid. I thought love was a burden you didn't want."

"Have I ever made you feel like a burden?" Tate growled in her ear.

Lara thought for moment and answered candidly, "No." She'd been a burden to her aunt and uncle, but Tate had never made her feel that way. "I think it was my own insecurities. I'm sorry. I almost left without telling you. I shouldn't have cared if you could love me back. I should have said it."

"It wouldn't have been the end," Tate told her firmly. "I would have come after you, used everything I had to make you want to be with me. Somehow, I would have worn you down eventually," he finished confidently. "I wasn't kidding when I said I needed you, baby. I would have lost my mind if there was no hope."

Her heart was so full of love that Lara thought it would explode. "I love you, Tate Colter."

"Christ, baby. I worship you. I adore everything about you. I don't know how you couldn't have known how I felt about you."

She leaned back and looked into his eyes. "Maybe because I was so head over heels in love with you. Fear is a powerful motivator."

"I wouldn't know," he teased. "I think the only thing that's ever truly terrified me is you leaving me." He grasped the back of her head, pulled her into him and crushed her mouth with his.

Chapter 15

He kissed her as though he were making a vow, as if he'd never let her go. His tongue swept into her mouth and he slanted his mouth over hers again and again, until Lara was out of breath and panting.

"I need to be inside you, Lara. Now," he demanded as he pulled his mouth from hers. His breathing was rough and heavy.

"Yes." She fumbled with her jeans frantically, needing him so desperately that it was painful. "Please, Tate."

They stripped at what was probably a record speed, a tangle of legs and arms, as they tore at their own clothes and each other's.

Lara's heart beat frantically, her breathing hot and panting as she looked at Tate, completely nude. She put her hands on his shoulders and ran her palms all the way down his chest and abdomen. "God, you're a beautiful man." She brushed her fingers over his hard, heavy cock and wrapped her fingers around him. "I can't believe you love me."

"Believe it," he answered in a low, desperate voice. "You're mine, Lara. You'll always be mine."

She couldn't argue with his arrogant comment. Her heart *would* always belong to him. She squeezed his cock gently. "Does that mean this is mine?" she asked seductively, loving the way his eyes flared as she teased him.

"Everything. This whole body is yours, flaws and all," he rasped. He slid his fingers down between her thighs and stroked through the wet heat that greeted him and groaned. "Mine. All mine," he said greedily.

"Then take it," she begged him, needing to feel him, be connected to him.

He kissed her hard on the mouth before he turned her body and placed her hands on the arm of the couch. She closed her eyes as she felt Tate cup her ass, and stroke over it roughly.

"Hold on, baby. I don't think I can hold back right now," he warned her in a husky tone.

"No holding back," she demanded, wanting him to take her rough, make her his.

She gasped as his fingers plunged between her thighs, stroking through her folds to tease her clit. He moved through her heat possessively, covetously. Two of his fingers dipped into her channel, curled around the sensitive place inside her that made her go completely insane. "Tate," she whimpered, needing him to make her come. Her body was tight and she trembled.

"Tell me, Lara. Tell me." He kept up his rough, sensual assault.

"I love you," she cried out, throwing her head back as he intensified the pressure to her clit, and fucked her with his fingers—harder, faster, stroking over her g-spot with every pump.

"Oh, God." Her body convulsed.

"Come on my fingers, Lara. Let go," he commanded.

She didn't have much of a choice. Her climax hit her hard and fast, intensifying as Tate removed his fingers and impaled her with his cock. His groan of ecstasy had Lara rocking back against him. She clenched the fabric of the couch as she felt her body coil tightly again.

"I can't come again," she panted wildly. Everything was so intense, so overwhelming that she was certain she'd break apart.

"You can and you will," Tate growled as he fisted a hand in her hair and pulled her head up. "Look at us."

Lara's vision was blurry with leftover tears, but she stared across from her and saw a sight so carnal, so erotic that she nearly came just from watching Tate's face. The full-length mirror propped up against the wall showed both of them; Tate pummeled into her with unrestrained lust. She watched, entranced as her breasts jerked and swayed with every thrust of Tate's hips. The carnality of feeling and watching them at the same time made her pant even harder, her eyes glassy and fixed mostly on Tate. He looked like an ancient warrior claiming his woman, and the sight was so raw that it ramped up her desire even more. "Harder," she whimpered. The sight of Tate mastering her body, his fingers pulling her hair erotically was so damn good. The sensual image would be burned into her brain from this moment forward.

He thrust harder and buried himself deeply inside her with every stroke. Lara moved her ass back against him; their skin slapped together as they both reached their breaking point.

Tate *was* going to make her come, and she wasn't certain she'd survive it.

He released her hair and trailed a hand along her back. Lara kept her head up to watch his every movement; his face contorted in both anguish and pleasure.

"Mine," he declared roughly. He met her gaze in the mirror, and their eyes locked together.

"Yes." She nodded her head, keeping her eyes locked with his.

One of his hands slid down her belly, searching for and finding her clit. He grasped it roughly and rolled it between his index finger and thumb.

Pleasure and pain ripped through her, the feeling so intense that it sent her body into a powerful climax.

"That's it, baby. Come for me," Tate insisted dominantly.

She imploded as if her body responded to his commands. The walls of her sheath spasmed wildly and her reaction was so strong that she dropped her head, breaking eye contact with Tate.

"Pull your head up. I want to watch you," Tate growled. He tilted her head by her hair again. "Watching you come is the sexiest thing I've ever seen," he groaned as he pounded into her.

"I love you," Lara screamed.

"I love you, too, baby," Tate answered in a strangled voice, and pumped into her one last time before he found his own release.

They shuddered together. Tate's arms wrapped around her waist as the last ripples of her climax faded. "Jesus, you will kill me. But I'd die this way anytime," he whispered low and heated in her ear as he leaned over her body. His chest heaved as he swung her around and picked her up, carrying her over to the big bed and collapsing, protecting her fall with his body.

She climbed off him so he could breathe, and then snuggled up beside him. He grasped her hand and entwined their fingers together as they caught their breath.

"Why do you have a cabin out here in the middle of nowhere?" She stroked her hand over his powerful chest, unable to stop herself from touching him.

"I don't," Tate confessed. "It's Gabe's. He uses it during fishing season. I asked him if he could set it up for me and if I could borrow it for a while."

"It's pretty nice for a fishing cabin." Lara looked at the beautiful rugs on the polished wood floor, the nice furniture, and she was already lying on the comfortable bed. "How far are we really from the main highway?"

He rolled on top of her and pinned her hands over her head. "Why? You planning on making an escape?" He sounded as if he was only half joking.

"No. I was just wondering if we have enough food to get us through the storm."

Tate laughed, a happy sound that filled Lara's heart with joy.

"I should have known you'd be worried about food." He grinned down at her. "I got us covered. Gabe had the caretakers make sure we were completely stocked."

"I suppose I'm cooking." She released a joking, beleaguered sigh.

"You'll teach me." Tate still smiled at her.

That dimple gets me every time.

She reached up and ran a loving finger over the indentation in his cheek. "Only if you want to learn. I really don't mind. I like to cook."

"I do want to learn. What if you're sick and can't cook? What if I need to take care of you?" His expression was anxious.

She smiled up at him. "You're not exactly short of funds. You can hire someone."

"Nobody will ever take care of you except me," he told her adamantly. "I'll learn."

Lara didn't tell Tate that she didn't need anybody to take care of her. His declaration had been too sweet, too tender, and it made her heart flip-flop.

She watched curiously as Tate slid off her and swaggered completely naked toward the door. It was very difficult for her not to focus in on his perfect, tight ass as he moved. He reached into the pocket of his jacket that hung on a peg, took something out and came back to the bed.

He looked almost sheepish as he knelt beside the bed. "I got this soon after the terrorist scare at the airport. I guess it will tell you just how long I've been crazy about you."

Lara's breath seized in her lungs as he handed her a tiny velvet box. She exhaled and popped the lid with trembling fingers. "Oh my God. Tate."

"Marry me, Lara. Stay with me forever."

In the bed of velvet was the most beautiful ring she'd ever seen. It was an enormous center stone diamond in an antique-inspired setting, which she was fairly certain was platinum. Smaller diamonds surrounded the center stone in a lovely circular setting. "I don't know what to say."

"Say yes," he answered immediately in a voice that was both demanding and hopeful.

"Yes." She looked up at him, her eyes filled with tears. He'd loved her almost from the beginning, just as she'd loved him.

Tate accepted her, actually adored her exactly as she was, and she felt the same way about him. They'd fight because they were both bullheaded, but they would also love.

He took the ring from the box and slid it onto her finger.

"It fits. How did you know what size to buy?"

"I told the salesman that you had beautiful, long slender fingers that almost make me come every time you touch me." Tate's expression was deadpan.

She slapped his shoulder playfully. "You did not."

He shrugged. "I guessed. I remember buying a pearl ring for Chloe when she graduated from college. I tried to judge from her size. We can take it to be sized if you need something different or you don't like it."

Lara sighed. "I love it." The diamonds sparkled and reflected the light as she turned her hand.

Tate grimaced as he climbed onto the bed and examined her hand. "Maybe I should have gotten bigger diamonds."

"You'd better be kidding," Lara said, amused. "Any bigger and I'd need a crane to hold up my hand." She rolled into his open arms and snuggled up against him.

"I want everyone to know you belong to me," he said obstinately.

"Don't worry. They'll know. I'll be your wife. And nobody could possibly miss my beautiful ring. Thank you."

"Thank you," Tate replied.

"What for?"

"For loving me," he answered huskily as he wrapped his arms around her tighter.

Lara wrapped her arms around him. "Chloe is getting married soon, and I don't want to take away from her happiness. She's been planning for a long time. Do you think we could just elope?" she asked Tate hopefully.

Honestly, she was secretly hoping that Chloe's wedding would never take place, but it sounded like a good excuse to elope.

"You deserve your day, baby."

"I don't really like weddings. I don't like the crowds, the noise, all the focus on the bride and groom. Honestly, my dream wedding would be over in under ten minutes," she admitted.

Tate pulled back to look at her face. "Seriously? You aren't just saying that because Chloe is getting married?"

Lara nodded. "Honestly. I don't want a fancy wedding. I know you're a billionaire and the Colters are a prominent family. If it's expected, I'll do it—"

"I never do anything because it's expected." He grinned at her. "And I hate weddings, too. Jesus, you really are my kind of woman."

"Vegas?" she suggested.

"As soon as the weather clears," Tate agreed cheerfully.

"I guess we'll have to find something to entertain ourselves until then."

"The storm is coming in. No outdoor entertainment, but I'll do my best to keep you well occupied." He winked at her and shot her a naughty glance.

"I think I'm starting to get bored indoors already," she told him mischievously.

"I'll get on that problem right away." Tate sounded amused as he lowered his mouth to hers tenderly.

He cured her boredom immediately, and so thoroughly that she didn't have another moment of indifference the entire night.

Chapter 16

It wasn't until the following afternoon that Tate found out that Travis had been right…again. The flight that Lara was scheduled to be on to return to Washington had crashed as it was taking off due to equipment failure. There were no survivors.

Tate watched Lara's face as she tried to absorb how close she had come to dying. His own heart raced as they watched the solemn news report.

Neither one of them had bothered to get dressed, and he wore a pair of pajama pants that he'd found in the closet, probably Gabe's. Lara wore a pair of warm cotton, pink pajamas. He'd hiked to the helicopter after he got up this morning to get her bags.

"Oh, my God," Lara gasped, her hand over her mouth in horror.

Tate looked at the television in the living room that he'd just turned on, wishing he hadn't. Lara would have had to find out eventually, but it hadn't needed to be today. She'd been so happy, so playful. They were still wallowing in the joy of finding out they were in love.

Oh, hell.

"It crashed, Tate. My flight. Everybody died," she said in a shocked voice, her eyes glued to the television.

He sat down next to her on the couch and wrapped his arms around her to cuddle her against his chest.

"I know, Lara. I know." Tate was practically hyperventilating himself, imagining how he would feel right now if Lara had been on that plane, and feeling sick for the passengers who had been on the aircraft. He could very easily been one of the people who were mourning loved ones right now.

"Those poor people." Lara started to cry.

Tate flipped off the news, unable to watch Lara's horror anymore. "Let's not watch it anymore."

Lara nodded, but she still sobbed.

He rocked her body against him, so damn grateful that she was here, alive and breathing. "I owe Travis...again."

"What happened last time? I'm so sorry I didn't believe you."

Tate shrugged. "I can't say I really believed it either when Trav first told me about his dreams. But a warning from Travis made me hesitate to take an extra mission. I only stopped for a minute because what he said kept running through my mind over and over. But by the time I volunteered for the extra operation, somebody had beaten me to it. Everybody on the mission died."

"So you understand how I feel," Lara murmured softly.

Yeah, he knew exactly how she felt: as if it should have been her who died, too. "I know how you feel, and everyone would have died whether you'd been on that plane or not. The fact that you survived doesn't make a difference to those people, so be grateful that you're alive and not feel guilty for living."

"Is that how you felt?"

He nodded. "Yeah. Except it should have been me instead of the other volunteer. It took me awhile to get over that."

Lara took a deep, tremulous breath. "I have to meet this Travis. He's amazing. I just wish he could have warned the airline."

"I'm certain he tried. But there's no way the airline is going to cancel a flight because some guy thinks he had a psychic dream. Most likely they'll just think he's nuts. This has never been a blessing for Travis. It's been more like a curse. It doesn't happen to him that often. And I don't think he's had a premonition dream since he saved Ally's life."

"Ally?"

"His wife now. You'd love her. She can bust Travis's balls when she wants to, and she used to be his secretary." Ally could wrap Travis around her little finger, just like Lara could do to him very easily.

"You're right. I'm sure we could be very good friends. Do you see them very often?" she asked curiously.

Glad that Lara was distracted from her near-death experience, he answered, "Not as often as I'd like. He lives in Florida. But we're both involved in the charity for abused women that I told you about. His brother Kade's wife is Asha, the woman who was abused, and started the charity."

"Travis and Kade Harrison?" Lara asked, her voice slightly awed.

Tate frowned, not particularly liking the fact that Lara sounded impressed. "You've heard of them?"

Lara snorted. "Who hasn't? Kade Harrison was a famous quarterback and a billionaire, and Travis Harrison is a brilliant businessman. I think it's great that they both contribute."

"We don't just contribute," Tate answered. "We run the whole operation. Jason Sutherland manages the financials and the rest of us do fundraising and other tasks that need to be done."

She pulled back to look at him. "Is every billionaire in America involved? Sheesh! Jason Sutherland, too?"

"Not all of them...yet. But we're working on it." He grinned at her, proud of the organization that all of them had formed to combat domestic abuse.

"I really would like to get involved," Lara mused.

"I offered." Tate knew now why she'd refused. "Now that you're going to be my wife, maybe you'll feel like you can be involved in any way you want to." He hesitated for moment before he added, "I don't ever want to hold you back from anything you want to do. I'd move to Washington if you want me to so you can continue to be an agent."

Fuck. That hurt!

The last thing he wanted was for Lara to put herself in danger every day as an FBI agent. But he didn't want her unhappy either. He *would* stand beside her with whatever she wanted to do, but that didn't mean he had to particularly like it.

"I like Colorado," Lara admitted softly. "And we'd have family here."

Tate's heart swelled at the fact that Lara was going to consider his family as her family, too. It had been a long time since she'd had family who really cared. "You might find them a little overwhelming at times." Tate knew he did. In fact, sometimes they drove him bat-shit crazy. But he loved every member of his family fiercely and considered himself lucky to be part of the Colter family.

"Solitude is highly overrated," Lara told him thoughtfully. "I'd love to have family."

"Well, get ready, baby, because you're going to have a lot of it now." He paused. "So how are you going to feel about giving up your career? Or are you going to just transfer to the Denver office?"

Damn. That hurt, too. But I have to make sure she has all of her options. This has to be her choice.

"Well, I'm actually going to have a very rich husband, so I think I'll ask him if he's willing to support us for a while if I go back to school."

Tate let out a giant whoop. "Hell yeah, he would. He's loaded." He kissed her forehead. "I have to admit, I'm relieved."

She cocked her head and looked at him as she said, "Thank you for giving me the option to be free to do whatever I want, even though you might not like my decision."

"I'm perfectly happy with your decision," Tate told her enthusiastically.

"It's nice to know that you're going to be the type of husband who would stand by me no matter what I wanted to do with my own career." She cuddled back against his chest. "You're pretty special."

He didn't feel special at all. Selfishly, he wanted her out of the field, but...

"I want you to be happy," he told her earnestly.

"I know. I feel the same way. Are you going to tell me exactly what you still do for the government?"

Tate shrugged. "Not a lot, and it's not dangerous, but I still work for them on a consulting basis. If they're having problems with a particular Special Forces mission, I help them out. I don't go out in the field anymore. It's strictly strategy."

"So you're a warfare genius?" she teased.

"Actually…yeah, I am. I always have been. Strategy and covert missions are my specialty." He *was* good at those things, so why deny it? He'd never exactly been modest, and he wanted Lara to know who he really was, all of his strengths…and weaknesses.

"Are you going to tell me what you were doing in Special Ops?"

"Working?" he tried.

"Tate," she said in that warning voice that really turned him on.

What the hell; they *were* getting married. "The team I worked for doesn't exist to most of the military or civilians. You were right when you said it was extremely covert and some of what we did was actually black ops. You're the only one who knows. I couldn't even tell my family exactly what I did, so I went on letting them think I was a SEAL. I was recruited after SEAL training because they needed another pilot for their team." His woman had already been pretty damn smart and figured that out, but he confirmed it anyway.

"I'll never tell. I swear I'll take it to my grave," Lara answered solemnly.

Tate shuddered, her comment making him think about her near-death again. "Which better not be for a very long time," he grumbled.

"Do you miss being on active duty?"

He paused for a minute and thought about her question. "I did for a while. I lived for my job, just like you did as an agent. My team was as close to me as my brothers. We lived, slept, and ate together sometimes. Giving up that kind of job is like cutting off a limb. But it wasn't something I was going to do forever. I was restless for a while, but I was slowly getting over it, moving on little by little. Now I'm glad I got out because if I hadn't, we probably wouldn't have ever met."

"And the crash that broke your leg?"

"It was a pretty risky mission. We got shot down before we could accomplish our goal. I was damn lucky I could land the helicopter without it going up in flames. But we took the impact pretty hard. I got most of the damage. Everybody else got out under their own steam." The whole operation had been screwed up, but at least nobody had died.

"Who got you out?" Lara asked anxiously.

"My team. They had to eventually carry me for miles before we got recovered."

"You actually let them carry you out?"

"It was either that or bleed to death in hostile territory. Right about now, I'm pretty damn glad I survived."

She eyed him suspiciously. "Did you take the damage intentionally?"

Tate shrugged, not really wanting to tell her that he had been willing to take the fall—literally—for the men on his team. He had tried to make the impact occur on his side of the copter near the front of the aircraft. "I was the senior officer and commander." He didn't really answer her question, but a look of dawning comprehension moved over her beautiful face, and made his admission unnecessary.

Their eyes locked together, and Tate felt as if he were drowning in her love for him. His chest ached as she looked at him as though he was everything to her…the very same way he knew he looked at her.

He covered her mouth with his because he had to, needed to. He'd come close to losing her forever, and he would have been a broken man without her. He shoved his hands under her pajama top, needing to feel her warm, silky skin under his fingers. Then, he lifted his mouth from hers and gently removed her cotton pajamas, touching and kissing every inch of skin that he revealed, worshipping her body just like he cherished her heart.

He stood and got rid of his pajama bottoms, grinning at Lara as he revealed no underwear. Tate stood there for a minute. His eyes roamed over her naked flesh; her long, tangled blonde locks of hair that floated around her shoulders; and then at her face.

She bit her lip. "Fuck me?" she requested.

He lowered his body onto hers carefully, knowing she had to be sore from their rough mating the night before. He smoothed the hair back from her face and trailed a finger down her cheek. "No, baby. I'm going to make love to my fiancée right now." He took her left hand, kissed his ring that adorned it, and then entwined their fingers together. He took her other hand and did the same thing, letting their conjoined hands rest above her head.

Lara instinctively wrapped her legs around his waist. "I love you so much," she whispered. Her eyes filled with tears.

Tate thrust forward and groaned as he felt her sheath accept him, welcome him with wet heat. "I love you, too, Lara. I always will."

He savored every moment of being inside her, having her surround him with her love. There was no rush as he entered her again and again, grinding against her with every pump of his hips. They moved higher and higher together. Tate tried to taste every exposed inch of her skin, relished the feel of her short nails as they dug harder into his back as she climaxed.

He buried his face in her hair as the walls of her channel clenched around his cock and massaged it exquisitely until he couldn't hold back his release. He came with a groan as he spilled himself deep inside her. *Mine.*

He held her possessively, protectively, damn grateful that he still had her with him. Things could have gone much differently, and he swore he'd never take her love for granted. Everything could be gone, lost in just an instant, and nobody knew that better than he did. He'd treat every day with Lara as a gift, because it was.

"Tell me something you really want—anything at all. I want to give you something," Tate said desperately, wanting to show Lara how much she meant to him.

She pulled his head back by fisting his hair gently. "I have everything I want, Tate. I have you."

Somehow, he didn't see himself as a very big prize. "What else?"

Studying his face for a moment, she finally answered, "Well, I did just turn thirty. I'd like to have a baby sometime in the next few years. I think I'll probably need your help and your consent since we'll be married."

Tate's heart went into double time. A baby? He hadn't thought that far ahead, but he could imagine Lara ripe with their child, rocking a daughter or son to sleep. Playing. Laughing. Loving. It would be amazing.

"I'd love that. A girl with your beautiful eyes and smile would be incredible."

"A boy with *your* eyes and your cute little dimple," she corrected.

"One of each?" It sounded like a good compromise to him.

"Babies don't exactly come made to order," she teased, squeezing his fingers as her laughing eyes smiled at him.

"I'm a Colter. We never give up." Hell, he'd give her as many babies as she wanted to have, and he'd love every one of them fiercely. "Dad tried until he finally gave Mom her girl."

"I'm not quite sure if I want to try as many times as your mom did for a girl, but we'll see. So I take it I have your agreement?"

"Yep. And you know I'm going to help just as much as you'd like." He'd help several times a day if she wanted to get pregnant. In fact, he'd help even if she *didn't* want to get pregnant.

"I think I'm going to need to practice until you're ready. A lot."

Lara snorted with laughter and pulled him back down to kiss her.

He obliged very willingly. This was one mission where Tate knew he'd have absolutely no reservations.

Epilogue

"What if she changed her mind? What if she doesn't show up? Maybe she figured out that I'm really an asshole?" Tate Colter looked at Travis Harrison with a panicked expression as they stood in the small wedding chapel in Vegas.

Travis crossed his arms in front of him and lifted a brow at Tate. "Colter, she already knows you're an asshole. I told her. But for some unknown reason, she still wants to marry you. She'll be here." Travis pulled back the sleeve of his custom-made suit to look at his watch. "For Christ's sake, it's only just noon."

Tate looked at his watch again. "It's one minute after," he corrected Travis gruffly.

"She's with Ally, and I'm pretty certain my wife isn't going to run away. I got over that awhile back. She loves me," Travis said arrogantly.

"Lara loves me, too," Tate said cockily, trying to shake off his nerves. He should have stayed with Lara just in case she got cold feet. Instead, he'd gotten ready with Travis, and Lara went with Ally to get a new dress.

Even though they were marrying in Vegas, Tate still wanted to make sure that their wedding day was special. He was dressed in a tuxedo, and Travis wore a suit. Luckily, Travis and Ally had been available to come and stand up for him and Lara. He'd thought about his brothers, but it was appropriate that Travis be his best man. He'd saved Lara's life, and Lara had wanted to meet him. He doubted his brothers would mind. None of them were in town this weekend anyway, so he could use that as an excuse. Plus, they all hated weddings just as much as he did.

Except...I really don't hate this one because it's my wedding to Lara.

In fact, he was really, really eager for it to actually start.

Another minute passed and Tate started to sweat.

Where in the hell are they? How long did it take to buy a dress?

"Maybe I should call her," Tate told Travis as he looked at the smiling chaplain, who didn't look as if he was in any type of hurry. And he probably wasn't. He was being very well paid for his services.

"No, you do *not* need to call her. Ally would have called me if there was a problem," Travis answered nonchalantly. "Lara isn't going anywhere. It's pretty evident that she's crazy about you. Relax."

Easier said than done. Tate felt like pulling his hair out.

He and Lara had only been living together for a couple of weeks. Had he done anything wrong? Okay. Yeah. He forgot to put the toilet seat down...occasionally, but he was getting better. Hell, he'd even learned to make a decent sandwich.

He thought that Lara would enjoy Vegas, and she had. They'd arrived several days earlier to see the sights and Lara loved the slot machines. But the thing she loved the best were the buffets. Tate grimaced when he thought about all of the buffets they'd found... some of them decent, but most of them absolutely disgusting. The only awesome buffet he could think of was the breakfast buffet served at the resort. It was quality food prepared by an excellent chef. Apparently, Lara didn't notice the difference and was entranced just by the large quantity of food. But he'd had so much fun watching Lara flitting from dish to dish that he didn't mind going. She'd stuffed herself until she could barely get up and walk, and every day she swore she wasn't going to do it again. The next day, she'd be seeking out another all-you-can-eat smorgasbord.

Christ...she was adorable. Lara was his heart, and she was going to be his.

If she would just get here!

Rationally, he didn't think that she was going anywhere. She *did* love him. He knew she did, but he wasn't going to be happy until they had said their vows.

He looked at Travis and wanted to punch his friend's smirking expression.

"You'll get over this irrational fear eventually." Travis sounded amused. "In time, you'll only start worrying about her ten times a day instead of twenty."

"Are you at ten yet?" Tate asked hopefully.

"Nope. But I'm working on fifteen," Travis answered sheepishly. "It's not easy loving somebody that much, but it's worth every minute of worry you'll ever have. Trust me."

"Are you worried now?" 'Cause honestly, Tate felt pretty terrified.

"No. Ally told me they might be a little late. When Lara found out that you were wearing a tux, she wanted to look nicer."

"She looks beautiful in anything," Tate replied emphatically.

"She's a woman," Travis answered, as if *that* explained everything.

"A female who can almost kick my ass," Tate said proudly.

"Exactly the type of woman you need, Colter. You need somebody who won't put up with too much of your bullshit."

"She doesn't. But I like that about her." He paused before he added, "Most of the time."

Travis laughed.

Tate looked at his friend, a man who had been so serious, so stressed and anal not so long ago. Now he looked relaxed...and content. "Are you really happy now, Trav?" Tate asked him seriously.

"More than I ever thought I would be, buddy. And you will be, too. Lara is a fantastic woman, and she's perfect for you. She wants to meet Asha now so she can see if there's anything she can do even before she goes back to school. She wants to help. Your woman has a good heart," Travis told Tate sincerely.

Tate nodded. He knew the extent of her heart, and it was as big as the ocean. "I know. I just wish she'd stop hugging on you for saving her life." One time Tate had tolerated okay, but it seemed as if Lara was always grateful to Travis every time she saw him. And he didn't care whether Travis *was* his best friend; he still didn't want to see his fiancée hug another man under the age of eighty.

Travis raised a questioning brow. "Possessive much? I remember not so long ago that you really enjoyed jerking my chain with Ally."

Tate flinched, remembering how he'd flirted with Ally just to piss Travis off because he thought it was funny. He wasn't laughing anymore. "I regret that now," he grumbled.

Travis smirked. "Good. Then I'll stop telling Lara how much I appreciate hugs of gratitude."

Tate glared at Travis. "You didn't."

Travis shrugged. "I might have mentioned it."

Bastard! Travis had intentionally made sure Lara threw herself into his arms in gratitude every time she saw him. "Do it again and I'll make sure I hug Ally for a very long time every time I see her," he warned Travis.

"I'll stop," Travis said hastily.

He's still crazy about Ally.

Tate smiled because he knew Travis would love Ally until he took his last breath. As much as he loved to tease Travis, the guy deserved that kind of love and Tate couldn't be happier for him. Especially since he was lucky enough to find the same kind of love himself.

Uneasy, Tate glanced at his watch again only to realize that it was only five minutes after noon.

Dammit!

Travis elbowed him in the side. "Take a breath, buddy. Your bride has arrived."

Tate looked at the entrance eagerly, disappointed when he saw only Ally. But Travis's wife looked ravishing in a very light lavender dress that floated around her calves. Her blonde hair was piled on top of her head; little ringlets curled around her temples.

Tate watched as Travis moved down the aisle, kissed his wife, and whispered something into her ear that made Ally blush. He offered his arm. Ally took it and let Travis bring her to the front of the chapel.

Ally squeezed Tate's arm as she passed and smiled at him as she took her place across from where Travis had stood a moment ago. Because Travis and Ally were their only witnesses, Trav was doing double duty. He was not only the best man, but he was also escorting the bride.

Travis walked back down the aisle and offered his arm again, and Tate's breath expelled hard from his lungs as Lara stepped up to his side. He sucked in another breath, feeling as if he'd been sucker-punched as he got his first glimpse at Lara, beautiful in a white and lace dress with three-quarter length tight sleeves and a fitted bodice. She held a bouquet of red and pink roses, and her hair was up. She had a small circlet of silver on her head that had a small, old-fashioned veil down the back.

She looks like an angel.

Her smile was radiant as she walked down the aisle toward him, her gaze focused on his face.

Mine.

He took her hand as she arrived with Travis and clasped it possessively, twining their fingers together as he took a deep breath.

She's here. She's mine.

The service was short, just the way they both wanted it. Tate spoke his vows reverently, and meant every one of them. Lara repeated those vows, her eyes on him as she promised him forever.

It seemed as though it was over so quickly, but Tate let out a breath of relief as they were pronounced man and wife. He definitely kissed the bride longer than necessary, and all four of them left the small chapel and got into a waiting limo.

"That was lovely," Ally said enthusiastically from her seat next to Travis.

Lara beamed. "It was. It was exactly what Tate and I wanted. I'm so happy that you could both come for the ceremony."

Travis popped the cork on a bottle of champagne and they all laughed as they jumped from the sudden burst of sound.

He poured and passed the glasses around.

Tate looked at his bride, thinking what a lucky bastard he really was. Lara had blasted into his life when he least expected it. He'd been so damn lonely, and he'd never really known it...until her.

He leaned over and gently kissed her temple. "You look incredibly beautiful, and I love you so damn much it's killing me."

She threaded her fingers through his. "Is this going to require revival then?"

"Hell, no. I'm plenty...alive. Every bit of me," he told her mischievously. "But I'll pretend I'm fading if you want."

She giggled like a young girl. "I love you, too." More seriously she said, "You make me so happy that it's scary."

Tate knew exactly what she was feeling. But he'd calm her fears. It wouldn't be long before that happiness was a constant state of mind for both of them.

"A toast," Travis announced. "Here's to marriage, love, and finding the person of your dreams."

The clink of glasses was loud as they all heartily agreed and took a sip of the fine Cristal.

"I guess we'll all be doing this again soon for Chloe's wedding." Ally leaned back in her plush seat.

"Are you guys coming?" Lara asked excitedly.

Ally nodded. "Yep. Chloe is very fond of Travis."

"I'm glad we won't have to wait long to see you again," Lara told Travis and Ally happily.

Tate's mind drifted to Chloe and how unhappy she'd seemed lately. He reminded himself that he had some work to do to dig into her situation with James. Something about their whole relationship didn't sit right with him. And after what Lara had said about James acting like a dick at the gym, he wasn't exactly thrilled about Chloe marrying somebody who could possibly not treat her right. Now that Tate knew what real happiness was like, he didn't want anything less for any of his siblings.

"Hey, Ally. There's that buffet I was talking about," Lara squealed.

"Let's stop." Ally nodded her head eagerly. "I'd love to try it."

Travis sent Tate a pained expression. Obviously he was about as fond of Vegas buffets as Tate was. And unfortunately, Ally seemed to adore them as much as Lara did.

"I'm a billionaire. We can eat at any restaurant in town. Do I really need to suffer through a buffet?" Travis said loftily.

"Yes."

"Yes."

Ally and Lara both answered Travis's question.

"This is Lara's day, Travis," Ally told her husband firmly.

"We can afford a regular restaurant, Lara." Tate confirmed Travis's opinion.

"But I'd love to go." She shot him a longing look.

"You want your wedding dinner to be a buffet?" *Oh, God help him.*

"It's lunch. Ally and I will let you and Travis pick where we go to dinner."

Ally nodded in agreement with an eager smile.

Tate looked at Travis again, and Travis just shrugged. He looked back at the look in his new wife's eyes and caved almost instantly. "Let's go," Tate agreed. He didn't think he could ever deny his wife anything, considering she asked for basically nothing but his love.

He reached into the inside pocket of his tux, pulled out a roll of antacids, and popped one into his mouth before he handed them over to his friend.

Travis took three before he handed them back to Tate.

"The things we do for our wives," Travis grumbled good-naturedly.

The women basically ignored the men as they chattered.

"Yeah, but they're worth it," Tate said with a grin.

They pulled up to the curb of the casino with the ladies' buffet choice.

Travis helped his wife out of the car and went ahead of them. Tate pulled his bride out of the limo carefully, steadying her as she tilted on her high heels.

"I know you hate buffets, but I'll make it up to you later," Lara whispered in a sultry voice into his ear so only he could hear her. "Ally took me to a lingerie shop, too. You'll like what's under the dress better than you like the wedding dress." She winked at him playfully.

His dick was as hard as diamonds as he contemplated what the hell she was wearing underneath her dress.

I'll make it up to you later.

Hell, maybe he *could* learn to love Vegas buffets.

He offered his arm to his wife and she took it with a wicked grin.

It was the first time that Tate Colter had ever entered a gigantic cheap buffet with a huge smile on his face, but it definitely wasn't the last.

Tate ended up being very happy with the arrangement, and never again complained after their wedding night, and Lara making it up to him. Eating the bad, mass-produced food had been more than worth it considering what he got in return.

Travis wasn't exactly bemoaning his fate either, because Ally had been to the same lingerie store as Lara.

They were back at another buffet late the next morning, both men armed with antacids and a huge grin on both of their faces. Both men looked very eager to make any sacrifices required to keep their wives happy after a very good night.

Tate had learned very early in his marriage that sometimes compromise was well worth the reward. His wedding night had been spectacular, but the greatest prize in their bargain was very simple: seeing his wife smile.

~The End~

Please visit me at:
http://www.authorjsscott.com
http://www.facebook.com/authorjsscott

You can write to me at
jsscott_author@hotmail.com

You can also tweet
@AuthorJSScott

Please sign up for my Newsletter for updates,
new releases and exclusive excerpts.

Books by J. S. Scott:

The Billionaire's Obsession Series:

The Billionaire's Obsession

Heart Of The Billionaire

The Billionaire's Salvation

The Billionaire's Game

Billionaire Undone

Billionaire Unmasked

Billionaire Untamed

9/16

Made in the USA
Lexington, KY
17 June 2015